for Magdalena from David

SEVEN
FOR
THE HALE AND HEARTY

David Z Crookes

ATHENIS HIBERNIAE
MMXXIII

The author is grateful to several editors who have allowed him to publish his work in its present form. Early versions of the first six tales appeared long ago in PRAESIDIUM and in FOMRHI QUARTERLY. The original version of I WANT CLOTHES appeared in INTELLECT ENCOUNTERS FAITH (Cambridge Scholars Publishing, 2014).

Cover photograph by Ethan McFerran

All rights reserved. No part of this publication may be reproduced, stored in a retrieval system or transmitted, in any form or by any means, electronic, mechanical, photocopying, recording or otherwise, without the prior permission of the author.

Printed in 2023 by Shanway Press,
15 Crumlin Road, Belfast BT14 6AA

ISBN: 978-1-910044-52-0

© 2023 David Z Crookes

This book is dedicated to Miss Katie Kennedy,
who last year graduated with first class honours in law.
Katie appears on the front cover as an
example of a hale and hearty reader.

THE TALES

First tale: UNDER THE EARTH

Second tale: BEHIND THE TOWER

Third tale: ON THE WIND

Fourth tale: PILLOW-TALK

Fifth tale: THE OLD PRETENDER

Sixth tale: TOTAL WAR

Seventh tale: I WANT CLOTHES

First tale: UNDER THE EARTH

AT the moment Delia is exercising outside in the dark with a hula hoop of stainless steel.

Do you abominate mad stories that start in the middle? Then let me explain. Delia Benn is a well-known actress and dancer. She lives happily with her parents in the house next door to mine. Delia has published five articles on Shakespeare in academic journals. On Saturday night she will be dancing the rôle of Principal Persian Slave in Musorgski's *Khovanshchina*. I was invited to help with the creation of a poster for the opera. 'Do a semidigital dream-painting of Delia,' said the concert manager. 'I want to fill every seat in the house.'

We should really go back a little. After graduating in classics, Delia took a course in creative writing. I was her main tutor for that course. Once she gained her MLitt, she became my friend and model. Over the last four years I have painted her more than one hundred times. Nearly every night, between ten and eleven, all year round, if she isn't working, Miss Benn exercises either in my back garden or in her own. Her decorous gymnastic uniform comprises a half-top and shorts of dark blue canvas. I never watch her. Our neighbours are unable to see her, with the exception of one person whom you will meet soon.

On the stroke of eleven Delia comes to take me for an hour-long walk. At that time of night I am always at work in the painting shed which fills a corner of my front garden. (Something in me refuses to call it a 'studio'.) Before we go for our walk, Miss Benn puts on the light cotton raincoat that she keeps in my shed. When we get back she makes a modest supper for both of us, either in her own kitchen or in mine. The moment at which a flushed euphoric Delia walks from one of our back gardens round to my painting shed is the moment at which she is seen by a particular neighbour, whose curious character may no longer be concealed.

Callisto Poon lives across the street from us. Although she refuses to believe that 'nubile' is a real English adjective, Callisto maintains an internet blog called NUBILE (= No Unconscious Bias In Local Education). Miss Poon calls herself 'The Watchdog'. Many educators call her 'The Warthog'. Last year Callisto accused me of being 'a heterocratic Hammurabi'. Yesterday she described me as 'shamelessly pulchritudinist'! Miss Poon loves to denounce the 'vestimental exploitation' of lady tennis-players. (Delia has a tennis-court at one end of her garden.) Once a fortnight, The Watchdog warns her readers to avoid 'a certain theatrical maidservant of toxic masculinity'. And every night, at ten fifty-five, she appears on her verandah, holding a short telescope. What impact does Delia's Olympian purity make on her dank and sullied mind? Don't ask me.

It's five past ten! For the last seven hours I've been at work on a painting of the Blue Lough (a sternly beautiful lake in the Mourne Mountains, near Annalong). Now I need to find my grafting-knife, which a friend called Pete Stodie wants to borrow. I ought to be starting a new picture, but I've eaten only three pears and a banana since my late lunch at three o'clock, so I'm not thinking about art. I'm thinking about Hatim Tai's Chip Shop.

Let me tell you a bit more while I search for the knife.

Pete Stodie is fifty-four years old, and seventy-six inches tall. He lectures in the Latin department of a respected university. He also chairs the local gardening club. His parents live in a fishing village called Ardglass, less than thirty miles from Belfast.

Pete's wife Gera is forty-two years old, and seventy-three inches tall. Ten years ago she gave up modelling, acquired an MA, and began to illustrate children's books.

Pete and Gera have twenty-year-old twin daughters called Caroline and Cornelia. Each of these ladies is seventy-five inches tall, or three inches taller than Delia Benn.

I'm quite old, and six feet tall, but the Stodies make me feel like a teenage Zacchaeus.

Although I have known the Twins well for three years, the idea of painting them has never occurred to me. Caroline and Cornelia are both students of mechanical engineering. They are better known as fanatical builders of boats and huts. When they don't have to be somewhere else, the Twins are nearly always in cold water. From January to December you will find them together in ponds, lakes, rivers, and the sea – either swimming, or sailing some bizarre craft of their own creation. 'I cannot fathom those *eel-bodied* girls,' their Aunt Stella once told me. 'I think they must have swallowed tapeworm-eggs. They eat like horses, and yet they look like bean-poles. They could be famous models like their mother if they didn't refuse to wear indoor clothes. Why are they both obsessed with gyroscopes and free energy? I wonder what will become of them. Every day they run for miles, and work out with weights. They have no interest in normal things like television, make-up, fashion shows, parties, candlelit dinners, or boyfriends.'

But the Twins excel in useful areas of life. One of their professors told me last month that Caroline and Cornelia are both heading for first-class degrees. In addition, the Twins have become nourishers of their own church. Last year an inspired vestry put them in charge of the junior Sunday school which a pair of weak-minded Trendy Babes had almost ruined. (The tittering Babes had really only two passions in life: their own squalid 'worship band', and some television programme called *The Simpsons*.) Today the reborn Sunday school is characterized by disciplined study of the Bible, by the singing of proper hymns, and by healthy honest laughter. I ought to say that when the Twins attend church, or university, they wear severely cut costumes of washable black cloth, made by themselves.

Caroline and Cornelia refuse to wear what they call 'the Maoist fatigues of the witless West', or blue denim trousers. They also refuse to wear clothes that can't be washed.

'Suppose you spend £220 on a go-to-work-in suit that needs to be dry-cleaned six times a year at £12 per time,' Cornelia said to me once. 'Then suppose the suit lasts you for ten years. You'll spend a total of £720 on getting your suit cleaned, so it's really costing you £940. That is *ludicrous*. It's like paying a high rent for a house that you're supposed to have purchased. All clothes should be washable. Most people are unbelievably stupid.'

The Twins are always making things. Last year, using an electric hacksaw and a welder, they ran a miraculous Art Nouveau bridge of mild steel across their garden pond. 'It looks rather delicate,' Aunt Stella complained. By way of response Caroline and Cornelia set twenty hundredweight bags of sand on the middle of the bridge. Of course the architectural expert made no apology. Such people never do. We all have friends or relations like Aunt Stella, and the marvel is that we don't murder them. But never mind! On the following day the Twins christened their new structure *Le Pont des Nymphes*, and asked me to make them a pair of shell-trumpets.

Every couple of months the four Stodies and I play as guests on the gender-neutral football team of a rural church. No harm in telling you. The so-called 'Psycho Twins', aside from being hideously fit, are feared by all. I mean to say, you have a fair chance of getting injured even if you play on their team. The bellicose doctrine which they expound on the field of battle would have sent Erich Ludendorff lurching over to the schnapps trolley. Last year Cornelia favoured our elderly referee with a smashing accidental knee-kick in the stomach, and knocked him out cold. That gentleman (a retired teacher of art, and Glebe Warden of the rural church) now avenges himself once every month by contributing a two-page strip-cartoon called *The Warrior Queens* to his parish magazine. Gera Stodie, who wrote her MA thesis on the graphic novel, was very impressed with the pilot episode.

Back to the present! Having located a beloved old grafting-knife, I leave it on the bench in my workshop. At right angles to the knife I set an ancient bradawl, whose beechwood handle is split. Two minutes later, beholding the state of my larder, I find myself sympathizing with a remote lady ancestor of L Ron Hubbard, so I walk over to a local convenience store. The cool salubrious night air makes me feel like an adolescent. In the store I am served by a man called Herdie Thistle, who works by day as a technician in the local art college. When I get home, I set out twelve items on the kitchen table: two turkey-and-ham dinners, two chicken tikka masalas, four portions of Russian salad, and four sticky toffee puddings. Before I can put these items in the fridge, my phone rings.

'Hello, dear.' It is Cornelia Stodie. 'Are you in bed?'

'Of course not.'

'Excellent. Caroline is here as well. Listen very carefully. A storm-drain runs past your house. Did you know that? Good. Well, the manhole-cover in the street right in front of your house sits over an access shaft, which has its own steel ladder. Caroline and I have lifted the cover from an altogether similar manhole about a quarter of a mile away.' (Cornelia tells me exactly where.) 'I've sprayed that cover with red aerosol paint in case you need to find it, and you know our blue car, which is parked in front of it. Caroline has already gone down the ladder, and I'm standing on the fourth rung, ready to let the cover drop down over us. We've attached lamps to our heads, and we're going to crawl along the drain as far as your house. What? Do you need to ask? *You* gave us the idea, dear! Yes, you did! Last Sunday, when you were in our house! You talked to Dad and Mum about II Samuel 5. 8! And no, we didn't think of telling you! Be serious. If we *had* told you about our Little Plan, you might have tried to stop us.' Cornelia pauses. 'I must let this cover drop. Please go out to your front garden, dear. You'll find a bottle of liquid disinfectant soap lying on your lawn. We left it there ten minutes ago. Put that bottle in your outdoor cold shower. And unlock the door of your workshop, so that we can use it as a changing-room. Then lift *your* manhole-cover, and wait for us to appear. Set a red flashing light beside the open manhole. If anything goes wrong, you know where we are. Each of us is carrying a generator of sound. By the way, we're both starving. We've eaten almost nothing since dinner-time. One last thing. Under your car you'll notice a white bag containing two large towels. Leave that bag where it is. See you soon, dear!'

After obeying Cornelia's unlikely commands, I change into an old tracksuit, and put on a pair of green wellingtons. Like a robot I turn on the oven. Then, standing by the open shaft, and hoping that nothing will go wrong, I begin to calculate.

What time is it? Ten thirty-five. A quarter of a mile is thirteen hundred and twenty feet. If the crawlers can maintain a speed of one foot per second, they should pass the imaginary halfway-post at ten forty-six, and they should be with me at ten fifty-seven.

Across the street, eighty-year-old Mrs Herring is going for a walk with Prince, her dignified dog. A well-polished brass plate on Prince's gate proclaims his mistress to be a Teacher of Ballet. Mrs Herring was born in Murmansk, and she once conversed with Vladimir Nabokov in Montreux! Tonight, in the lamplight, she looks only a little older than Delia Benn, her most famous pupil.

At ten to eleven, being unable to wait any longer, I climb down the shaft-ladder, and plant my booted feet in a stream of water. The music of the water is audible only at close quarters. Climbing down the shaft is like climbing up a tower in reverse, and hereby hangs a doleful tale. For some time I've been trying to purchase a little Victorian building in Ardglass called Isabella Tower. At lunchtime today I was told by a solicitor that the Tower can't be sold. 'There is a problem with the title deeds,' she said.

Never mind that! My feet are cooling down. Not a hint of human speech comes along the tunnel by way of reassurance. What's wrong? Why are the Twins keeping quiet? Suddenly I realize that the open manhole represents a danger to noctivagant beings, so I climb up again in order to keep vigil on the surface. Orange light from a street-lamp reveals the proximity of Callisto Poon, my anything-but-nubile neighbour.

'I might have guessed!' she cries. 'What on earth are you doing?'

'Nice of you to inquire,' I reply. 'Our storm-drain is being checked. Two of my friends are inspecting a quarter-mile stretch that ends here.' As I speak, two thrilling concordant notes sound from below. (A *d'* and an *f'*, played on shell-trumpets.) When Caroline calls a gentle *Yee-hoo!*, and begins to climb the ladder, I whisper a joyful *Alleluia*, and speak into the shaft. 'Many thanks for doing that job, ladies! My neighbour is standing beside me. She wants to express her own gratitude. We'll both be able to sleep easily tonight.'

But I wonder how easily Miss Poon will sleep tonight. One amazingly tall and exquisitely beautiful lady appears on the street, followed eight seconds later by an exact replica of herself. Each lady wears a beryl-green version of Delia's exercising costume. Breathing audibly, the two living pillars of innocence greet my neighbour. I replace the heavy manhole-cover. The Twins relieve themselves first of their head-lamps, and then of their shell-trumpets, which hang on canvas neck-straps. I turn off the red flashing annoyance. Miss Poon puts her hands over her eyes, and murmurs something about *flagrant exploitation*.

'Ignore that daft woman,' I tell the Twins. 'While you two are getting washed, I'll make the supper.'

After handing me her car keys, Cornelia warbles into a tiny phone. 'Oh, are you both home, Dad? That's good. A Family Friend has been helping us with a job. We're at his house now, and we haven't eaten yet, so we'll be late.'

Valkyries with Velcro, forsooth! Callisto winces eight times, like an electrified blancmange, as the Twins remove their thick knee-pads and oversized gardening gloves. (It's funny. Mrs Herring wears identical pieces of armour whenever she weeds her front rose-bed.) At length, growling something about the *longicrural lackeys of Nordicentricity*, Callisto staggers away. Caroline and Cornelia regard her with incredulous horror.

Miss Poon's expensive watch bleeps twice.

Bearing a silver circle, effulgent Aphrodite makes her entrance. (Delia is a close friend of the Stodies, partly because Pete was her Latin tutor for three years.)

In the same moment Mrs Herring appears on the pavement. 'The Judgment of Paris!' she cries. Her corgi stands panting on the kerbstone, with his tongue floating in air. Cornelia pats the dog. Miss Benn asks what has been going on. Caroline tells her.

'Well, I am *jealous*,' says Mrs Herring, one minute later. Her eyes of emerald green flash in the lamplight. 'I wish you had invited me to participate in your mischief! Good night, dears.'

Delia puts one arm around old Mrs Herring, and leads her across the street. Then the two women commune gravely for most of a minute. I can't hear what they're saying, because noisy acts of ablution are being performed behind me.

What now? Aphrodite is approaching the manhole! Carefully she raises its cover, sets it on the street, and disappears into the shaft.

Feeling like a mere puppet of history, I microwave one of the turkey-and-ham dinners. Seven minutes later I place it in the ordinary oven. Once the microwave is addressing dinner number two, I exchange boots for running shoes, and canter off to collect the Twinmobile from Redpaint Street. On my return I find Delia sprinkling brown sugar over a plate of sliced nectarines. As the microwave squeaks to announce that a second dinner is ready, two tracksuited nymphs enter the kitchen, glowing and exultant.

'We have a present for you, dear,' says Caroline. 'It was *acquired* on Rockall. Please don't ask us any questions.' Cornelia gives me a cocktail sausage of granite. I go and fetch the grafting-knife.

Refusing chairs because they want to straighten themselves, the Psycho Twins stand and destroy the steaming turkey-and-ham dinners, along with the Russian salads. When I point to the tikka masalas, Cornelia says *Yes, dear, and the four little puddings as well*. Miss Benn is content to make pot after pot of tea.

At one point I notice the three girls conversing discreetly. Are they talking about Women's Business? Like washable black costumes? No. Aphrodite is commanding the Twins to leave their gloves and knee-pads in the back yard, so that she may disinfect them. Selfless creature!

At length Miss Benn and I find ourselves alone.

'The food-bill for tonight's little tale is nearly twenty pounds,' I observe sadly.

'Don't complain, dear!' says Delia. 'You've got a tiny bit of Rockall.' She regards me thoughtfully. 'You've also got a tale that you can publish, word for word.' She pauses. 'Once the tale is over.'

'What do you mean? The tale is over.'

'Wrong.' Miss Benn strikes a Junonian attitude. 'It's about time that *I* appeared in a short story, and I don't want to make a cameo appearance, so deeds must yet be done.' The goddess commits a theatrical act of inhalation. 'Listen! I *always* do my own stunts. By making a great effort, I can lift our millstone of a manhole-cover with two conjoined pairs of fingers. You'll be able to lift its twin with two fingers.' Juno pauses. 'Furthermore, when I stand on the fifth rung of our shaft-ladder, I can raise the manhole-cover, not without difficulty, from inside. You'll be able to raise it quite easily.'

If the chronicler of these events was a cartoon-star from *The Warrior Queens,* I know what he'd be saying now. GULP!

'Do try to speak, dear,' says Juno, who has gone back to being Aphrodite.

'Very well.' The subterranean world is taking over my life. 'Tell me something at once. What are we going to do?'

'We're going to find the manhole which the Twins used as their starting-point. You can drive, dear.' Delia looks over with yearning at the plate of nectarines. 'Have you had dinner yet?'

'No.'

'Neither have I.' Miss Benn groans. 'Never mind! We'll climb down the shaft, replace the manhole-cover, and crawl along the storm-drain until we come to our own shaft. I've hung my walking-coat from the last-but-one rung of our ladder, so whichever of us goes first will brush into it in the dark.'

'In the *dark.*'

'Oh, yes. Then tomorrow you and I will be able to say, *Caroline and Cornelia, we have surpassed you!*' Delia flexes her long entrancing arms. 'Come on, dear. The gloves and knee-pads are outside. Let's not utter a word until we're safely back. By the way, there'll be three of us.'

Miss Benn and I leave the house.

Some Fiendish Female Golem from *Sinister Tales* is dancing a mazurka on the pavement. She wears hockey shoes, gardening gloves, knee-pads, a balaclava helmet, and a navy-blue boiler-suit.

It is Mrs Herring.

All three of us get into my car. I drive slowly for less than three minutes. We get out of the car. I lift the red-painted manhole-cover. Delia and I put on our gloves and knee-pads. Mrs Herring enters the shaft, followed by Delia. After twenty seconds I enter the shaft, and replace the heavy, hateful, hostile manhole-cover.

We climb down the ladder in complete darkness.

We crawl along the storm-drain in complete darkness.

Mrs Herring goes first.

Delia goes second. The aura of clove-carnation perfume which enfolds her, even after an hour's hard exercise, persuades me that I'm not dreaming.

A balletic fact strikes me in the audible presence of water. On Saturday night my fragrant neighbour has to stand on one spot and dance, with her fingers interlocked behind her neck, before doing a gymnastic backward flip. 'It will be a wonderful discipline for you!' Mrs Herring has told Delia.

'Forty-eight years ago, in Moscow, I had to do exactly the same thing.' Musorgski's opera Хованщина (*Khovanshchina*) is not a bag of laughs, but its title deserves to be pronounced properly. Say *Kh* like the *-ch* of 'Bach', say *shch* like the *-sh ch-* of 'cash cheque', and make the four syllables weak-strong-weak-weak, as in English 'anàthema'. Хованщина was formerly translated 'The Khovanski Affair'. Since the mid-1970s it has been rendered 'Khovanskigate'! Many readers will know the opera's miraculous prelude, 'Dawn on the Moscow River'.

For some reason the wordless rhythm of our journey helps the time to pass. I fear that our lead crawler may suffer a heart attack, so the music of the culverted stream passes me by. I think of II Samuel 5. 8, the verse which the Twins adduced in connection with their latest exploit. You can read that verse in your own time. David's men had to make their way up a kind of vertical sewer. Down here is a lot more pleasant: all horizontal, and no unfragrance.

Suddenly two good things come together into my mind – the ancient bradawl that I told you about, and the little sausage of granite that the Twins gave me. Last year a dear friend from church left me the bradawl in his will, along with a collection of rare saws, chisels, and planes. Some of the planes are more than a hundred years old. Now the bradawl needs a new handle, and the granite sausage needs a useful function. In my painting shed there lives a so-called pebble tumbler. Its electric motor causes a little barrel, no bigger than a large paint-tin, to revolve slowly. You half-fill the barrel with pebbles from a river-bed, or from a beach, pour in enough water to cover them, and add one tablespoonful of a particular grit. Then you switch on the motor, and get on with your life. To turn the pebbles into polished stones you need three different 'spins': seven days with coarse grit, fourteen days with medium grit, and five days with fine grit. The beautifully polished stones which appear after twenty-six days are visual and tactile delights. I decide to put my piece of Rockall in the tumbler along with a number of river-pebbles from Annalong. (I'll use a diamond-tipped drill to make a hole in the polished sausage for the tang of the bradawl's blade. Then I'll repair the old beechen handle, and use it for something else.)

But hey! After what feels more like ten than twenty minutes, Mrs Herring's head meets the hanging coat.

We climb up our own shaft-ladder. I go first, Delia goes second, and Mrs Herring, who has forbidden us to help her in any way, brings up the rear.

When, with unballetic awkwardness, I overcome the sullen gravity of the manhole-cover, and force it to slide on its way, grating and begrudging, fierce orange light dazzles my eyes. I emerge to find Callisto Poon standing on the pavement.

'Hello again,' I mutter. 'Thought we needed a second look at the drain.' I remove my gloves.

'Double-checking,' Miss Benn explains brightly, taking her stand beside me. 'Had to be done.' She removes her gloves, and drops them on the ground. 'You can't inspect a storm-drain too often.'

'Black vice!' wails Miss Poon. 'Black vice!'

'You want to see what my neighbour has got in his workshop,' says Delia, widening her eyes prodigiously, and speaking in the voice of a brainless bimbo. 'My neighbour has got a big BLUE vice.' She bends down quickly, and tears off her knee-pads. 'My neighbour has also got a small RED vice.'

'Aaaagggghhhh!' shrieks Callisto. Mighty dread has seized her troubled mind, for a Thrice-Dead Thrall of Darkness is rising inexorably from the manhole.

'Oh, stop getting on like a demented old maid,' says Mrs Herring, who has come to the ladder's third rung. 'You should have played rough games in your youth, Miss Poon, but I suppose it's too late now.' She sits on the street, and swiftly withdraws her legs from the shaft. 'All hellish doctrine and no healthy exercise makes Jill an unwholesome girl.' Mrs Herring rolls gracefully on to one padded knee, and stands up. 'I had to have this talk with you.'

Not far away, with inexplicable viciousness, someone turns a key three times – forward, back, forward -- in the old-fashioned rim-sash lock of a back door. Then Callisto's elderly cats move painfully toward us. All three of them suffer from arthritis, and no wonder. Miss Poon compels her three guardians to exist on a diet of soda bread and lemonade.

As a dog barks quietly, the octogenarian Teacher of Ballet embraces first Delia, and then me. 'That was *tremendous* fun,' she says. 'I thank God for his protection, and I thank you both for your tolerance. Let me detain you young people no longer! I am going to do what I used to do in the days when I was a ballerina, and lie in a hot bath for an hour.' Mrs Herring pauses. 'Tomorrow morning I shall write boastful letters to all my silly depressed friends. Good night, dears.'

I replace the manhole-cover.

Wagging his tail ecstatically, Prince comes over to lead his mistress home.

With rapture I rip off my knee-pads. Mrs Herring was right. I am a Young Person, but Callisto Poon is an Old Maid!

At length the Unwholesome Girl goes to her own place, walking like a spiritual love-child of King Agag and Mrs Grundy.

Delia and I run round to Redpaint Street. I bring a can of black aerosol paint with me, and spray the manhole-cover. We drive home.

Miss Benn fills a large enamel bucket with water from my outside tap. She adds a tot of amber antiseptic, creating a white liquor in which our epic shoes, gloves, and knee-pads will steep overnight.

Once we have disinfected ourselves and bathed in cold water, Miss Benn and I come out of our respective houses, arrayed in clean tracksuits. Both of us have been strengthened by an underground adventure that involved a certain element of anxiety. Both of us are glad to walk upright in the open air.

For more than a mile two small bats provide us with a flying escort. Even in a fallen universe, there is genial fellowship.

'I've been thinking,' says Delia. 'We haven't *surpassed* Caroline and Cornelia.' She pauses. 'The Twins may have had head-lamps, but they did act as pioneers.'

'So they did. Thanks to the Twins, we three were guaranteed a safe passage in the darkness.'

'Correct. There might have been anything down there.'

'Yes. Like a grid blocking the drain at one point.'

'Or a dead animal.'

'Or a tangle of barbed wire.'

'Or *a great rat colony*.' Miss Benn strikes an attitude of mock terror.

The man who cycles past us is gabbling into a mobile phone. 'That's right! Grace's little book is overpriced, so it's going to end up in the bargain bin. Reggie? Well, yes and no.

We've sold a few copies of his race-gender-class book.' ('There must be some real saddoes about,' Delia declares.)

One twig from an old and kindly tree falls portentively at our feet. After picking it up, I examine it in the white light of a new street-lamp. The twig, studded all over and apparently budless, is a solid arc. It has the dark satin surface of a Jacobean oak wardrobe. Some unwritten text compels me, by the mere power of its will, to break the twig in two. I put the pieces in my pocket.

'Oooohhh.' My neighbour stretches herself luxuriantly. 'I am *starving*.' She touches her toes for a second, and stands up again. 'We'll eat the nectarines when we get back to your house, dear. Afterward we'll go out to the garden, and I'll practise my dance for *Khovanshchina*.'

'No, love, you'll do your dance first.' (With gladness I behold the open door of Hatim Tai's Chip Shop, where the girlie word *salad* is unknown.) 'It'll be hard enough for you to do a backward flip with a big fish supper on board.'

'That is sensible.' Miss Benn sounds faintly surprised. 'Have you anything more to do tonight?'

'Yes! I want to do a picture of Isabella Tower before I turn in.'

'No, dear. I've got a better idea.' Delia pauses. 'Thirty seconds ago, I had a Vision of You, doing something wonderful.'

'What was I doing?'

'You were painting a washed-out storm-on-a-coral-island dream-picture of Me, along with solid meringue-like wisps of morning mist, and petals, and leaves, and a couple of falling twigs.'

'Such a painting…...' I stop to think. (*Washed-out* means steeped in the sink, pressed between sheets of kitchen roll, dried in the microwave, and gone over with a hot iron.) 'Such a painting will take a lot of work.'

'It'll take you about forty minutes, dear, and you'll enjoy the work tremendously. I'll stay with you, and keep you from falling asleep.'

Some Lawless Weakling roars past us, at about fifty miles per hour, in a canary-yellow car. The Weakling appears to have throttled his silencer.

Musorgski holds no sway over the Chip Shop. Dolly Parton is singing 'Jolene'!

Delia whispers her own *Alleluia* as we approach the stainless steel counter. Each of us is a *Stammgast* here.

We order two fish suppers from Hatim Tai.

Then, turning our backs on the warm high counter, we look around happily, contemplating a piece of real knowledge, and wondering where to sit.

Seven feet away, like fearless yachtsmen, two gold-and-silver gyroscopes are hiking on the edge of a table.

At the same table two immaculate ladies, garbed in austere black costumes, are slicing up ten-inch pizzas.

'We are *bad*,' says Cornelia. 'I feel embarrassed.'

'We are *evil*,' says Caroline. 'I feel ashamed.'

'We really need to be *beaten*,' says Cornelia.

'So we do,' says Caroline, looking at me directly. 'Or in some manner *punished*. Let us tell you how, dear.' She glances at her sister.

The Twins create a kind of stage-oracle effect by speaking in unison. 'You can paint us,' they say.

'As often as you like,' says Cornelia.

'If you order a big ice-cream dessert for each of us,' says Caroline. 'Now.'

Bargain deal! I take a five-pound note out of my pocket. Then, as the Twins return to their victuals, Hatim Tai replaces 'Jolene' with the scherzo of Bruckner Eight, and for the first time tonight I think I've got some power.

The two untarnished gyroscopes are spinning away in a Dirac Sea of Tranquillity.

Radiant Aphrodite speaks in my left ear. 'Remember thou art mortal, dear.' She pauses. 'That applies to me as well. No boasting! We shall allow the Psycho Twins to believe that their latest exploit is unique.'

All right. For a while.

'Yes.' Delia smiles coldly. 'Until the tale of tonight is published.'

Second tale: BEHIND THE TOWER

HERDIE Thistle, an amateur occultist who works in the local art college, regards me with a mixture of curiosity and dislike. He manages to discover some dark hermetic subtext in everything that I write or paint. (Listen to what Mr Thistle told me last week. 'The first fourteen sentences of "Under the earth" contain a total of 666 letters.') Yesterday Herdie invaded my garden, and showed me a mostly-white photograph from the local paper. 'A model of Isabella Tower, made from sugar cubes!' he explained. (Isabella Tower is a little old building which I tried to purchase not long ago.) After noticing the aerial-wires that ran along my garden fence, Herdie began to talk about ley lines, Rosslyn Chapel, reptilians, and the Satanic cartography of Washington. When he revealed that CONVENIENCE STORE was an anagram of VIENNESE CONCERTO, I thought about murdering him with a great axe.

These dull thoughts afflict the chronicler while he acts in a *farce absurde*.

I am wearing academic dress over my football kit, in case anyone notices the viola-case. Delia Benn is wearing gold sandals, complicated calf-straps, and forearm gloves, along with a bat-girl half-top and shorts, so that any revellers who cross our path will stare at her, and ignore me. Both of us are masked. Down in the harbour Caroline and Cornelia, made up like Vampire Mermaids, have already attached listening devices to the hull of a happy-looking boat.

A former colleague of mine, who helps to keep everyone safe, is acting as project manager. Rockets are shooting up into the sky all around us. A new year has begun, and so has my second tale.

The tale really began two weeks ago. It was a dry windless night. Having completed a drawing of Greta Hegans, whom you have yet to meet, I was listening to the *Te Deum* of Berlioz. (Herdie Thistle used to have a murky mystical passion for Greta.) On the stroke of eleven, after exercising for an hour, Delia came into my painting shed.

'What a day!' she exclaimed. 'In the morning I had to address a group of illiterate ladies who believed themselves to be "feminist writers". They were all rather frightful – cropped hair, shapeless clothes, and oversized glasses. They spent their lunch-break ranting in ungrammatical English. Did you know that the *dénouement* is evil because it appeals to a male notion of pleasure?' The radiant Delia shrieked with laughter, and lifted her walking coat from its peg. In the same moment two high-rise delphiniums made an imposing entrance. Each delphinium wore a half-top and shorts of red canvas.

Caroline looked with approval at Delia's similar blue outfit, and spoke. 'You'll do the way you are,' she said.

Cornelia looked thoughtfully at my built-for-comfort ensemble of camouflage trousers, lumberjack shirt, and heavy pullover. At length she spoke. 'Go and put on your football kit, dear,' she said. 'Be as quick as you can. You should wear your running shoes.'

I went away to change, longing for a good feed of potatoes and kippers.

Four minutes later, three athletic girls and one footballer got into the Twinmobile. An enormous black object was moored to the roof-rack.

'Don't speak until we tell you,' said Caroline.

It was warm in the Twinmobile. Hoping that our journey would be long, Delia and I fell asleep. Sixteen minutes later we were brutally roused, and forced to get out of the car. We found ourselves on the Seafront Road in Cultra (pronounced Cull-TRAW). Already Caroline and Cornelia were removing hooked elastic ropes from their enormous black object. The object turned out to be a shallow dinghy, dark as a funeral scarf from stem to stern, as the cheerful Tennyson writes in *Morte D'Arthur*. Cornelia pointed three times: first to me, secondly to the boat, and thirdly to the pavement. I reached up and took hold of the dinghy. It was astonishingly light. At the bidding of Cornelia's right forefinger, I lifted the black vessel over the low sea-wall, and carried it down the concrete slope which rises from a narrow strip of beach. Caroline and Delia followed me. Behind them came Cornelia, bearing a black oar in each hand.

Still resenting the murder of my sleep, I marched into the sea, and committed our craft to the waves. When the dinghy was floating in twenty inches of cold water, I took hold of its stern with both hands. Caroline got in first, received the oars from Cornelia, and sat on the middle of the rowing-bench until Miss Benn was safely installed in the bow-seat. A street-lamp allowed me to discern that our vessel bore a nice reassuring name (THE ISLAND OF THE DEAD). Once Cornelia had joined her twin on the rowing-bench, I climbed aboard, and established myself in the stern-seat. Two sisters plied their black oars. As our dinghy glided gently on its course, I stopped hanging members of a press-gang from the imaginary yard-arm, because Delia was sending me a message in flagless semaphore. (IF MRS HERRING WAS HERE, SHE WOULD CRY *ARTHUR AND THE THREE QUEENS.*)

After about four hundred strokes of the oars, Cornelia spoke. 'Thanks for coming, you two! Our new hollow vessel is made entirely from sixteenth-of-an-inch plywood, and so are its hollow oars.' She paused. 'In each case we laid strips of plywood over a complicated ribwork of the same material. We cut all the bits and pieces to size on a bandsaw. After that our only tools were a glue-gun and a sander.'

'Is the plywood marine quality?' I asked.

'No,' replied Caroline. 'That's why we've given everything three coats of bitumen paint.' She and her twin shipped their oars, and sat astride the rowing-bench so as to face each other. 'Now listen, dear. We're talking here so that we can't be bugged or overheard.' Caroline paused. 'Delia's here because she knows what a catwalk is, and you're here because Dad has told us about The Work That You Used To Do. Listen to my sister for a minute.'

'Gather round,' said Cornelia, as from nowhere she produced a laptop computer. Miss Benn and I moved from our seats in careful concord. As we knelt by the rowing-bench, a male countenance materialized. 'This man is head of security in the university's department of mechanical engineering,' Cornelia explained. 'We'll call him Mr W. He has two mobile phones, but during his lunch-break he sometimes uses the payphone in an alcove of the lobby. One day we overheard him coming out with two sentences that I'll show you now.' Yellow words, set on a green background, replaced the pink face.

But it has always helped us, Herdie. A circle supported by an octagon has great occult power.

'Hold on,' I said. 'Are you certain that he said *Herdie*, and not *Herbie*?'

'Yes,' the twins replied in unison.

'Then we can identify Mr W's interlocutor,' I said. 'One of the banes of my life is a technician from the art college called Herdman Thistle. His friends call him Herdie. He was named after the Herdman Channel of Belfast Lough, and he claims that his forename is unique. Herdie is immersed in every imaginable species of verbal voodoo.'

'This exceeds anything which I could have imagined,' said Cornelia. 'Well done, dear.' She paused. 'We thought that Mr W might be involved in some kind of witchcraft, so we bugged the payphone, and waited for him to use it at lunchtime. Yesterday we managed to record a one-sided conversation. Read the transcription.' Cornelia pressed her PAGE DOWN button.

Here are the new orders. Same place. Once you get out of your taxi, strut as if you're on the catwalk. No furtiveness! Wear the fancy-dress costume that you used at Hallowe'en. Oh, and carry your festive lantern. I have to do the same. I'll leave the big taped-up viola-case with Lobelia Waters (Watters?) at precisely 11.53 pm on New Year's Eve. You must arrive there at precisely 11.59 pm. Pick it up, and leave as soon as the fireworks start to go off. A boat festooned with coloured bulbs will be waiting for you in the harbour.

Delia spoke. 'I reckon that Mr W is talking neither to Herdie, nor to any other man,' she said. 'He's talking to a woman. Men do appear on the catwalk, but in barbarian speech the verb *strut* is generally reserved for female models.'

(Miss Benn has done a good deal of modelling in her time.)

'The fellow's language,' Delia continued, 'is neither cold nor peremptory. Look at the word *festooned*.' She paused. 'Mr W is addressing a lady whom he likes. And when he says *I have to do the same*, he's treating the lady as an equal, rather than as a subordinate.'

'What about Lobelia Waters?' asked Caroline. 'Is *her* odd name genuine? Like the name of Herdman Thistle?'

'No,' I answered. 'Lobelia Waters isn't even a person. Mr W says *Same place*, and he tells his interlocutor to *arrive there*. He doesn't say *arrive at her house*, or even *be with her*. He says *arrive there*. So Lobelia Waters must be the codename of an exact location.'

'Water lobelia is a plant,' said Cornelia. 'It used to grow in Lough Neagh.'

'What does the viola-case contain?' asked Delia.

'Not a musical instrument,' replied Caroline. 'I mean, if the thing which had to be picked up was a priceless viola, made by Stradivari, it would be called a viola, and put in a case whose existence would be too trivial to mention.'

'So it would,' said Miss Benn. 'Does the case contain documents, then? Or a weapon?'

'I don't know,' answered Caroline. 'It would be rather jolly if we could find the place, and pick up the viola-case, before Mr W's accomplice arrives. Then we could go to the police.'

Cornelia regarded me in the darkness. 'You haven't said much, dear,' she murmured. 'How can we find out what Lobelia Waters means?'

'I'm not sure,' I replied. 'But I know how Herdie Thistle would address the problem. If we could get on the internet in mid-ocean…..'

'We can,' said Caroline, producing a large mobile phone from nowhere. 'Give me a moment.'

Laughter came to our ears from dry land. Merry persons were enjoying a late promenade.

'Fire away, dear,' said Caroline.

'See if you can find *Andy's Anagram Solver*,' I said. (Herdie's darling tool.)

'Is that ay-en-dee-wye-apostrophe-ess?'

'Yes.'

'Right.' More laughter from the shore. 'Got it! What shall I do now?'

'Ask the solver to give you two-word anagrams of LOBELIA WATERS. Spell WATERS with one tee to begin with, and see what happens.'

'OK.' After about twenty seconds, Caroline showed me the screen of her phone.

asteria bellow
bellow asteria

isabella tower
isabella wrote
isolate warble
lower satiable
orbital weasel
realisable tow
realisable two
satiable lower
tow realisable
tower isabella
two realisable
warble isolate
weasel orbital
wrote isabella

'Oh, ho.' I shivered with joy. 'Look at the third line, ladies.'

Miss Benn was first to react. 'It must be!' she said.

'What do you mean, dear?' asked Caroline. 'Is Isabella Tower the pick-up location?'

'Of course it is,' replied Delia. '*We* all know that Isabella Tower is a building in Ardglass, where your grandparents live. In Mr W's book, the important thing about Ardglass is that it has a *harbour*, where a boat will be able to wait.' She paused. 'One's neighbour took one down to see Isabella Tower not long ago! He wanted to buy it, but there was some problem with the title deeds.' Miss Benn inhaled slowly. 'Cornelia, can you go back to the first passage that you showed us on your computer?'

'Yes.' Cornelia struck her PAGE UP button. 'There you are.'

But it has always helped us, Herdie. A circle supported by an octagon has great occult power.

'What a sublime indiscretion!' said Delia. 'Isabella Tower has only two storeys. The lower storey is octagonal, and the upper storey is circular.'

'Ooohhh,' said Cornelia. 'That is *incredible*, Delia.' She closed her computer. 'Let's get back to the car. You and your neighbour can row. I'm going to look up Isabella Tower on the internet.'

Caroline spoke into her phone. 'Mum, two close friends of the family are helping us with a job. Don't wait up for us. Cheerio!'

Once we were back in the Twinmobile, I took over. 'Drive to Downpatrick, by way of Saintfield,' I told the twins, 'and head for Ardglass. Wake me up when you arrive.' I was tired, and Delia was falling asleep already.

Fifty minutes later, Cornelia shook me out of a glorious dream about old-fashioned English meat pies. 'Is that it?' she asked.

'Yes,' I growled, referring stupidly to a torch that some clown had placed in my left hand. Then I saw the Tower.

Four variously clad characters emerged from their vehicle, and walked for a short distance behind a dark line of modern houses.

We had reached our destination. A steep grassy path led to Mr W's occult power-house. The said path was blocked by a forest of brambles.

'Time for a bit of nocturnal horticulture!' said Caroline in a low voice. She ran back to the Twinmobile. From its arsenal of tools she brought a pair of garden shears and a pruning-hook. Subsequent events were beheld by Delia and myself from the relative safety of the lighting desk.

Several 'publicly available sources of information' exaggerate the dimensions of Isabella Tower, which consists of two tiny rooms. (The nineteenth-century nobleman Aubrey Beauclerk built the Tower as a place of convalescence for his daughter Isabella.) Early on the morning of 17 December, the building looked strong and innocent.

Now, early on the morning of 1 January, it appears not to have changed. Everything has gone well. At 11.35 pm a begowned footballer and a spectacular bat-girl concealed themselves behind Isabella Tower. At 11.53 pm a lantern-bearing Anubis left an oversized taped-up viola-case in the Tower, close to its only doorway. At 11.54 pm a begowned footballer took possession of this case, and replaced it with an apparent twin. (The taped-up twin contained a solid cut-to-shape block of poplar-wood.) Then the footballer rejoined the bat-girl. At 11.59 pm a lantern-bearing Nefertiti arrived at the Tower, and picked up the substitute viola-case. She made her exit to the accompaniment of fireworks and boat-horns. My former colleague is following Nefertiti down to the harbour. Bat-Girl and I walk back to the car. We meet only two persons on our way. (One is a Quiet Man. The other, his consort, is a latter-day My Fair Lady, who trays to speak polaytely. 'Pestor Cort-Rayte esked for ay Kendid Response, Ellick, so Ay said, "Pestor, thet new hymn-book is ay Payle of Crêpe." ') The black-lipped and blue-bodied Psycho Twins, now arrayed in green tracksuits, have done their unpleasant work without being detected. It is 12.15 am on New Year's Day.

I take off my gown, and roll it up. In less than a minute our weird quartet is on its way. My former colleague has asked us to take an appallingly devious homeward route, but I am able to relax. Someone else is driving. The car heater is roaring, the radiator in my painting shed has been on since nine o'clock, and a paradisal narcolepsy is waiting for my acquiescence. I remove my mask. What fascinating companions I have! Not long ago, the bat-girl who sits beside me played a minor rôle in *Khovanshchina* at the Belfast Opera House. People are still talking about Delia's performance.

On the main road, inebriated celebrators of the new year are posing for photographs in hackneyed attitudes of vulgar imbecility. They stretch out their arms, open their mouths, widen their eyes, and raise their eyebrows to the limit of possibility. Poor zombies! Idiots have taught them how to behave.

Two ghoul-faced maidens, a bat-girl, and a footballer get out of the Twinmobile at one thirty-five. Car-designers ignore the sonic dimension of door-closing, so the four little bangs that ensue are unavoidable.

As I feel for the key of my painting shed, mellow new-born light draws our eyes to an upstair window across the road. Callisto Poon, clad in pale pyjamas, is watching us through her telescope!

The shed is gloriously warm. I pull up the blackout shutter, which is made of marine plywood. Miss Benn removes her mask, and then fetches four pairs of polythene gloves from a little cupboard.

Caroline and Cornelia take off their masks. For a moment they stand in unwonted silence, surveying the shedscape with Bride-of-Dracula eyes.

'Listen, dear.' Delia is holding the viola-case in her gloved hands. 'I'll keep our Egyptian mummy parallel to the floor while you pull off its linen bandages.'

Four minutes pass while I strip away an eternity of parchment-coloured masking tape. Two efficient beings transfer every length of tape to the bin.

The entity that emerges is both inscrutable and importunate. When Miss Benn sets a lockless black viola-case on my painting table, I raise the catches, and lift the lid.

Inside the case lies a long trapezoidal box made of polished sheet brass. I take out the box. Tidy-minded Delia sets the viola-case on a vacant shelf.

The brass box is about three inches in depth, and forty-two inches in length. At its broad end it is nine inches wide, and at its narrow end it is four inches wide. I set the brass box on the table. Its top horizontal side, unlike its bottom counterpart, projects about a sixteenth of an inch beyond three of the four vertical sides. Is the top side a hinged lid?

Yes, it is!

Under the lid I expect to find some intricate piece of engineering, like the Antikythera Mechanism, but in the event my eyes are greeted by a number of beautifully wrought simplicities.

Ten lines of thin insulated wire run between twenty little black domes that are mounted on each long vertical side of the box.

'Like the crystal-set aerials on your garden fence, dear,' whispers the bat-girl, articulating my own thought even as I think it. (Should have told you that British *aerial* is American *antenna*.)

A ponderous paragraph of officialese has been laser-engraved in upper-case letters on the inside of the lid. Whoever wrote it has mentioned four expectable things: a certain university, its department of mechanical engineering, the British Ministry of Defence, and the British Official Secrets Act. I ought to feel intimidated, but I don't. By contrast, the dog that barks in a nearby garden sounds worried. Caroline mutters something about being starved.

Two pairs of bright golden strings, rigid as steel rods, are stretched about an inch above the floor of the box. The unequally long members of each pair are set half an inch apart. One pair is close to the left vertical side, and the other pair is close to the right vertical side.

Between the pairs of strings a narrow screwed-down copper block, about five-eighths of an inch in thickness, sits on eight one-inch-tall silver pillars. The top of this block bears an inscription: TUNING CHECKER AND DIRECTIONAL CONTROL. Bat-Girl hands me a large jeweller's screwdriver – brass-handled, blue-bladed, and exactly the right instrument for my present purpose.

With frank trepidation I extract eight fine-threaded screws. When I remove the twelve-inch-long copper block, which is much too light to be solid, I am confronted by a totally sealed system! Is the inscription a lie? Is the block an unfinished piece of work? Or is there something here that I can't see?

After screwing the block back on, I decide to measure the lengths of all four strings in millimetres. The left-hand long and short strings have lengths respectively of 1000 mm and 729 mm. The right-hand long and short strings have lengths respectively of 729 mm and 512 mm. ('All cubes,' Delia whispers.) Near the wide end of the box a little plastic wheel, about three-quarters of an inch in diameter, and a quarter of an inch in width, is set under each of the four strings.

Having examined the wheel which is set under the 1000 mm string, I try to make it rotate by brushing it with one finger. My attempt is successful, and surprising in its consequence, for the string begins to sing an opulent note, suggesting a mixture of bassoon and cello, midway between C natural and B natural. The little plastic wheel is behaving like the large wooden wheel that acts as a circular bow in a hurdy-gurdy. I wait for the wheel to stop moving, but it doesn't. Where is it getting its energy from?

While the 1000 mm string continues to sing, I activate the wheel which is set under its partner. The 729 mm string begins to sing an F natural. In terms of tone-quality and volume this note is a perfect match for the halfway-house note of the 1000 mm string, but for some reason the combination of the two notes is horrible.

Hoping that our inner ears will not be damaged, I activate the wheels that are set under the 729 mm and 512 mm strings on the right side of the box. These strings begin to sing respectively another F natural and a high B natural, the left-hand neighbour of a piano's Middle C. So hideous is the effect of the four strings sounding together that I close the lid of the box.

After a moment the polished brass box rises from the table, keeping its lid and bottom parallel to the floor. Within the space of five seconds it is pressing itself against the peak of the ceiling, as if it wanted to escape from us. The sound of its four strings has become tolerable. Am I the dupe of a delusion? No. Delia is biting her lower lip. The Twins are standing taut and motionless, like Josef Lorenzl statuettes.

I am enthralled. The amount of energy that I communicated to the machine, by activating its four little wheels, was negligible! Time to speak.

'How is it that the wheels are still rotating?' I ask. 'And where is the machine getting its energy from?'

'The engine which you kick-started with one finger, dear,' says Cornelia, 'is supplying its four wheels with energy siphoned from the atmosphere. That's what the lines of aerials are for.'

'Yes,' says Caroline. 'But the anti-gravity energy is being generated by the interaction of four precisely tuned notes.'

'Orpheus and Amphion,' whispers the fascinated bat-girl.

For thirty seconds all four of us look up at the brass box, and listen to its music. Then satiety engenders an advance. We have managed to start the engine. How may we stop it? I reach up, grasp the brass box in my right hand, and pull it downward, meeting a degree of resistance, as you might suppose. I set the box on my painting table, and lift the lid. Delia holds one hand over the middle of the box, so as to discourage it from doing another vertical take-off.

Ugly noise engulfs us.

Should I try to stop the wheels by using my right forefinger as a brake? Or should I use my right forefinger as a mute? The second idea strikes me as wiser, because it involves no rotating parts, and therefore no friction. I touch the 1000 mm string at its midpoint, and at once the wheel which is causing it to sound stops moving. That was easy! When I treat the remaining three strings in the same fashion, silence resumes her reign. The polished brass box is going nowhere.

'If an experiment is to be credible,' says Miss Benn, 'it must be repeatable.'

Correct.

In the course of the next ten minutes Caroline, Cornelia, and Delia do everything that I have done. Each of the three girls, working on her own, repeats the experiment.

Caroline fetches a camera from the Twinmobile, and creates a comprehensive photographic record of the engine. ('For what it's worth,' she says.)

At 2.30 am we put the brass box back in its case. I happen to be aware that the idea behind its motion comes from what people call 'a publicly available source of information', so I resolve to ignore the paragraph of officialese which is engraved on the inside of its lid.

Our project manager enters the shed without knocking. He brings five ten-inch pepper-ownie pizzas ('brave an well done', as we say), along with five lidded thermos-beakers of very hot tea. 'It must be wonderful to have *real power*,' says the ecstatic Caroline. 'We both love you, Mr Z,' says Cornelia. The Twins, Delia, and I unfold four stool-chairs. (These cleverly designed affairs spend most of their lives hanging like bats in one corner of the shed.) Newly-christened Mr Z takes my chair by the table. Some horrible cat squeals in a nearby garden. Once our pizzas are on their way, Mr Z asks affectionately after Mrs Herring, who in days of yore was his colleague. He goes on to tell us two things. First thing: Anubis, Nefertiti, and a fancy-dress Ancient Mariner – the sorcery-crazed garden-gnome agents of a friendly power – believe that they are working for Ordo Templi Orientis. Second thing: free energy is real.

Fifteen minutes of pure joy follow. Then Caroline and Cornelia wash five beakers in the tiny sink. We all wipe our fingers on sheets of kitchen roll.

My former colleague watches while Delia and I perform the experiment for a fifth time. At length, in the name of his ultimate superior, he urges me to divulge everything. ('Ordinary people *need* this bag of tricks,' he says, 'so we want competent engineers to start working at it, right away, all over the world. Here's a simple fact about modern life. Any such bag of tricks is *bound* to be stolen, sooner or later! Those who refuse to accept that fact are not patriots. They are idiots.') At ten to three our project manager tells us to keep the beakers, whispers ten syllables in my right ear (*I wish I had a clever team like yours*), and goes on his way, taking the machine with him. The Twins leave two minutes later – after ordering me to keep the beakers in my shed. It's wonderful to have real power.

Soon Delia leaves, unforgettably cross-gartered, bearing five empty cartons.

I push down the blackout shutter, and rub my eyes. A lacy-winged green insect is dancing on the window-pane. I feel old, weary, and utterly miserable. The lofty desire to comprehend an experience departs from me as lower satiable desires assert their power. I want a hot shower, pyjamas, a heavy pullover, thick trousers, slippers, and more tea. What kind of music sounds when I turn on the radio? What kind of speech, rather? *Akhnaten*! A formidable actor is declaiming sixteen words.

He GOES to the SKY, he GOES to the SKY, ON the WIND, ON THE WIND.

Someone taps on the door. I turn off the radio. A fourth muse, whom I have already named, is here to collect a picture entitled *Greta standing by a fire at night*. Or so I mistakenly assume.

'Hello, dear,' says Miss Hegans. 'I left a family gathering at two o'clock. When I reached Belfast I thought you might be working late, so I drove along your street, and saw the twins getting into their car. They said you were still up.' Greta pauses. 'I need to tell you a story that no one else will believe.'

To be continued, as they say.

Third tale: ON THE WIND

CERTAIN facts are not known to the whole world! Queen Victoria came to the throne in 1837. The word 'prehistoric' was used, perhaps for the first time, in 1832. Ardglass is a fishing village about twenty-eight miles from Belfast.

Let me throw another set of facts at you. Greta Hegans is a very tall MA student from the art college. She speaks in grammatical English, like Delia and the Twins. Last year Greta joined the Biblical study group which meets in my workshop. A month ago she bought an old mandoline, and began to restore it. Seven times, at her own request, I have created a pictorial record of Greta's athletic salubrity. (Last week I painted her as Calypso.) Every so often Miss Hegans contrives to fire some Brutalist Ceramical Creation of mine in the college kiln. On Christmas Day I gave Greta a copy of Feuillade's film *Les Vampires*. Today, at three o'clock on the morning of New Year's Day, Calypso has come into my painting shed – not to collect a portrait of herself, but to tell me a story.

'Behind our college,' Greta begins, 'and in the middle of what used to be a herb-garden, there is a large wildlife pond. The garden is overgrown with thistles and briars. A stream flows into the pond on one side, and flows out again on the other.' My guest glances for a moment at a framed photograph of two men. 'Before the Christmas break,' she continues, 'Herdie Thistle asked me if I would stand in the wildlife pond, wearing a swimsuit, and pose for a photograph. I was astounded! Most people are aware that the Thought Police of the art college abominate any depiction of womanhood. I mean, the reckless male student who paints a female form…..' Greta holds out two hands, by way of inviting me to finish her sentence.

'…..will be accused of "scopophilia".'

'That's right! Unless he declares himself to be "interrogating the gynocolonial clan kerygmas of the phallocentric hierarchy". And if he dares to take photographs of a lady swimmer, he will be denounced as "creepy"! I spend more than an hour every week modelling in a swimsuit for male students, but my work has to be done secretly, in the kiln-room.' Miss Hegans tries to suppress a yawn. 'Anyhow! Welcoming what I took to be a sign of rebellion, I agreed to be photographed by Mr Thistle. Now as you may recall, dear, Herdie used to have a weird numerological *thing* about me. He told me last year that in the numerical alphabet HERDMAN THISTLE added up to 750, while GRETA HEGANS added up to 474. Then he revealed that 750 and 474 were both "nonagonal numbers". Well, that was all harmless enough. But Herdie went on to confront me with an Occult Figurate Diagram, which proved that we were "congruent nonagons", and therefore destined to marry! I've never shown you this work of genius before.' Greta takes a sheet of paper from her valise, and hands it to me.

49

'I smacked his stupid head,' my visitor continues. 'Severely. Then I told him to go away and design a stealth bomber.'

'Occultism nearly always leads to mental disease,' I remark wearily.

'Indeed.' Miss Hegans looks over at the door for a moment. 'At the moment Herdie has a thing about your next-door neighbour. He keeps raving about her "controversial" performance in some Russian opera! I'm quite glad in a way. I mean, if he's thinking about Delia, he isn't thinking about me. But never mind. Back to Miss 474 posing in the pond. You won't be surprised that I drew up a pretty rigorous contract for the shoot! At no point would either of us address the other. There would be no greetings, and no shouted commands. I undertook to stand for five minutes in the middle of the pond, starting at precisely two o'clock on the afternoon of 30 December. My photographer had to make three promises. First, he would not arrive before me. Secondly, he would take only one picture. Thirdly, he would leave at four minutes past two. Well! Herdie duly consented. Then he said nervously that he was hoping to develop his photograph in a rather primitive manner. I asked him what he meant. He replied that Cicely Grove had got him interested in "undigital rusticity".'

(Cicely Grove is a fifth muse of mine, whom you have yet to meet. But what is *undigital rusticity*? Fingerless yokeldom?)

'I wasn't bemused, dear, although you seem to be.' Greta smiles. 'Cicely likes to employ old-fashioned cameras, and kitchen-sink chemistry. Whenever she develops her own photographs, she uses undecaffeinated instant coffee, powdered vitamin C, washing soda, and household ammonia. On rare occasions she uses ordinary salt as a fixer, instead of ammonia.'

'What kind of result does she get?'

'Oh, her results vary. On a bad day, Cicely will create an enchanting blend of blotchy cappuccino. On a good day, she will create a ravishing impressionist sepia from the late nineteenth century.' My visitor pauses. 'Last month you published a painting of the Twins, holding up a hollow steel mast in wonderful Côte d'Azur light. Miss Grove has turned your painting into a curious photograph.' Greta takes a picture from her valise, and sets it on the table. 'Here are the seventy-five-inch Flying Dutchwomen, standing on the crenellated stern of their ghostly vessel. As they leave the Island of the Dead, they hold up *nothing*. Furthermore, Dead People on the Island say farewell by letting off wonderfully synchronized flares.' My visitor laughs merrily. 'You may not like the photograph, dear, but it has created a fierce demand! Every male student in the college wants Caroline and Cornelia to model for him.'

Miss Hegans regards me soberly. 'Let me introduce you to another character.' She pauses. 'Herdie and I arranged our Lady-of-the-Lake shoot in the kiln-room. We were overheard by a nice-looking final-year student called Tony

Fisher. Tony is one inch taller than I am, and a bit older. He did two years of voluntary work before he started college. Last year he kept asking me to go out with him! I always refused, because Tony to some extent exemplifies the snorkelled fogeyism of the academic art-world. He admires Aubrey Beardsley, wears a blue velvet jacket, grows his fair hair far too long, drinks civet coffee, carries a *Swan Lake* crossbow, takes no exercise, and lives in an overheated indoor world.'

'Is my shed too warm for you?'

'No.' Greta feels in her valise. 'Here we are! Early in October, after firing a lot of ceramic hexagons, Tony got me to kneel behind the world's first-ever *tile-serpent*, and photographed me. He skilfully arranged his two-dimensional snake so as to hide both parts of my swimsuit.' Miss Hegans laughs. 'We were caught together by a lecturer called Amos Fleech, who appeared to radiate approval! Tony explained that we were interrogating the gynocolonial clan kerymas of the phallocentric hierarchy, but Amos told him not to worry about that nonsense.'

Fifty yards away, some thug sounds his car-horn in villainous valediction.

'Within two days,' Greta goes on, 'Tony had portrayed me as Eve. "You have been set ablaze by the serpent!" he said. "Your whole body is riven with desire. You feel fettered by the statute which has been imposed upon you. As you close your eyes to divine light, you yearn to engage with the forbidden tree." ' Miss Hegans hands me a photograph. 'Look.'

Expecting to see a piece of Obsessive Student Art, I am hit for six – or 'gubbed', in local parlance. If Tony Fisher's *Eve* deserves to get ten out of ten, and it does, then no picture of mine deserves to get more than three out of ten.

'As well as painting *La Scène du Serpent*,' Calypso continues, 'Tony has composed "Anatomy of Perfection", a poetic catalogue of my body parts, which runs to one hundred and five lines.' She pauses. 'Last month "Anatomy" appeared in a respectable poetry magazine. It is very well written, and perfectly decorous, unlike the reworking of Robert Louis Stevenson which Mr Fisher sent me on 18 November.' My guest produces a strange narrow postcard, and sets it on the table. 'Read that quatraine.'

I obey. Not far away, some vagrant cat gives a loveless gurgled scream.

> *I have one black arrow under my belt,*
> *One for the grief that I have felt;*
> *That one is for Miss Greta Hegans,*
> *Whose chill disdain is my own chief grievance.*

After twelve seconds, Greta speaks. 'What do you think of it?'

'It sounds dangerous,' I reply. 'Did you complain to anyone about the poem?'

'No, because I felt sorry for its author.' (Blue light – from an ambulance? – flashes in the street.) 'You see, during the summer holiday Tony lost a good deal of weight, and much of his mental stability as well. According to Herdie, Mr Fisher has stopped eating.' Greta shivers. 'When I was leaving the kiln-room on Christmas Eve, Tony brushed past me, muttering something about "one black arrow". And here ends the first part of my saga! Time for Exhibits B and C.' Calypso produces first a large album, and then a wrapped solid object. 'Attend, dear!' She lays the album on her chair. 'You are about to meet Lady Beryl Petalston.'

'Who was *she*?'

'My great-great-grandmother.' Greta begins to unwrap the object. 'Her grandson, who was my great-uncle, often used to allege that I was the exact image of Lady Beryl. I ignored his allegation until last March, when I inherited a miniature portrait of my ancestress, painted by Maria Eliza Simpson. I have here a blown-up photograph of the miniature.' My tall model, who is still standing, reaches me a small framed picture. 'What do you think of it?'

I study the likeness for twelve seconds before I speak. 'Lady Beryl must have been a woman of rare pulchritude. One can see what your great-uncle meant.'

'Thanks, dear!' Greta relieves me of her picture, and sets it on the table. 'In her first season she was regarded as a formidable beauty, although the slenderness of her arms was unfashionable.'

'Late Victorians liked the kind of arms…..' I almost manage to murder a yawn by talking through it. 'That Delaroche gave to Lady Jane Grey.'

'So they did! And it's odd that you should mention our Nine-Day-Queen, because my great-great-grandmother was supposed to have modelled her own intellectual and spiritual life on that of Lady Jane.' Greta pauses. 'Before she was twenty she could read and write fluently in six different languages, including Latin, Greek, and Hebrew. She studied the Bible assiduously. She played the organ in her family chapel for an hour every day. She painted flowers, and birds, and animals. I should add that she was an accomplished archeress, a respectable carpenter, and a fearless rider to hounds! It's a shame that no photograph of Lady Beryl has survived. She married at the age of twenty-two, spent her honeymoon in Ardglass, and died in childbirth one year later. After her death, the family fortunes went steadily downhill for three generations. Today my great-great-grandmother's only memorials are a tomb in Ashburton, a miniature portrait, and an illustrated album or commonplace book, which I inherited along with the portrait.' Calypso pauses. 'This album, unremarkable for its period, as at first I thought, contains a multitude of handwritten poems, cryptograms, short pieces of music notation, and watercolour sketches. I leafed through it in March, and set it aside. Three days ago I decided to examine the album properly. It turned out to be a record of things that Lady Beryl had seen or heard, between the ages of nineteen and twenty-one, *in her dreams.*' My guest lifts the album, and passes it to me. 'Take a look at the final page, dear, and then study the first three pages.'

I obey. A square of letters is printed in yellowy-brown ink on the last page. (When I was about ten, I made ink of the same colour from oak-galls.)

        C O L L E C
        T E D V I S
        I O N S O F
        L A D Y B E
        R Y L P E T
        A L S T O N

On page one, the text of Luke 13. 4 (*Or those eighteen, upon whom the tower in Siloam fell, and slew them, think ye that they were sinners above all men that dwelt in Jerusalem?*) is followed by a square arrangement of four consecutive words (THE TOWER IN SILOAM). I try to discern what is going on. The sixteen-letter square must be read from top to bottom, and from left to right. Letters five, nine, and thirteen are written in hard-to-read yellow ink. Letters ten and fourteen are written in jade-green ink. Letters six, eleven, and fifteen are written in bright blue ink. Letters one, two, three, four, seven, eight, twelve, and sixteen are written in glowing red ink.

```
      T H E T
      O W E R
      I N S I
      L O A M
```

I hear a dull critic murmur, 'The fantasy alternative of a con artist!' But the cryptogram will disturb any thoughtful reader who takes the trouble to examine it.

On page two of Lady Beryl's book, the forty-nine letters of an obscure message are set out both in a square table and in a quatraine.

A	S	O	N	A	T	H
R	O	N	E	A	R	E
M	O	R	B	I	D	I
L	L	S	B	I	D	L
A	W	N	D	E	P	O
N	E	A	W	A	R	D
E	D	W	I	L	L	S

As on a throne
Are morbid ills,
Bid Lawn depone
Awarded wills.

British readers who recognize that Lady Beryl is using the verb DEPONE here in its old sense of DEPOSE will perceive that her cryptogram relates partly to the Abdication Crisis of 1936. King EDWARD resolved to marry WALLIS Simpson (AWARDED WILLS = EDWARD + WALLIS). Stanley BALDWIN (= BID LAWN) was Prime Minister in 1936. The word HEIL is spelled by red letters seven, fourteen, twenty-one, and twenty-eight. HEIL combines with green letters six and thirteen to spell HITLER, whom Edward admired, and whom on one occasion he met.

What next? Something less colourful. Staid liturgic unity marks page three of the book, on which two poems are set out side by side – first in compressed square tables, and then in sets of quatraines.

```
THRIVINGBRAMBLESF
LOURISHNEARTHESEV
EREDSTREAMIWHOONC    AMIDSTYOURHEN
EDIDPERISHNOWCOME    RESIDESMYCLUE
BACKINDREAMTHOUGH    CHILLCODEDPEN
MYDISTANTDAUGHTER    TROLLDRESSEDI
MAYNOTHEARMYCRYIW    NBLUEMADUGLYR
HOSEETHEFUTUREWIL    HYMECOMEDUTYG
LNOTLETHERDIEGRET    OPAYHUNGRYTHY
ACALLSFORBERYLTHI    METHEIRPETALS
STLEGROWSAPACEWHE    KNOWWHATLITHE
NYOUSTANDINPERILI    GIRLBUILTMYLU
SHALLTAKEYOURPLAC    TEPEARLGREYJO
EUNIMAGINEDCLOTHI    INCOSMICQUILT
NGCHASTELYIEMPLOY    THEAUTHORSWAY
DUTYQUELLSMYLOATH
INGDUTYGIVESMEJOY
```

Thriving brambles flourish
  Near the severed stream;   Amidst your hen
I, who once did perish,   Resides my clue;
  Now come back in dream. Chill coded pen,
                               Troll dressed in blue.

Though my distant daughter
  May not hear my cry,
I, who see the future,
  Will not let her die.

Greta calls for Beryl,
  Thistle grows apace;
When you stand in peril,
  I shall take your place.

Unimagined clothing
  Chastely I employ:
Duty quells my loathing,
  Duty gives me joy.

Mad ugly rhyme!
  Come, duty, go –
Pay hungry thyme:
  Their petals know.

What lithe girl built
  My lute pearl-grey?
Join cosmic quilt,
  The author's way.

'Page three worries me,' says Greta. 'The long poem contains my Christian name. It also contains a STREAM which is SEVERED by the wildlife pond.' She pauses. 'It even contains a THISTLE that may be a proper noun.'

'HERDIE is there as well. Look at the end of the second stanza.'

'Golly.' Calypso shudders. 'How did I miss that?' She rubs her eyes unhappily. 'Never mind. I can handle myself and Herdie Thistle, dear, but I can't handle Tony Fisher.'

'Is *he* in the poem?'

'He is! And I found him only because you gave me an old French film for Christmas.' Greta takes the print-out of a screen-shot from her valise, and hands it to me. 'In the third episode of *Les Vampires*, Guérande decodes a cryptographic table. First he writes down the four corner-letters – top left, top right, bottom left, and bottom right.

'Then he writes down the immediate horizontal neighbours of the four corner-letters. After that he writes down the immediate horizontal neighbours of *those* neighbours, and so on. Do you temember?'

'Yes.'

'Well, on 27 December I treated THRIVING BRAMBLES in the manner of Guérande. Once I had written down the ten letters T F I Y H S N O R E, I stopped. The ten letters didn't spell anything plausible. Suddenly, as in Feuillade's film IRMA VEP turns into VAMPIRE, T F I Y H S N O R E turned into TONY FISHER. I thought that I was having a nightmare, generated by the film!' Greta pauses. 'I've gone as far as I can go. If you're not too weary, dear, you should look at Lady Beryl's two poems for thirty minutes. You're bound to see things that I haven't noticed. Will you oblige me?'

'Of course. What are you going to do?'

'Sleep.' Calypso sits down, folds her long arms, and closes her eyes.

Cryptanalysis is like riding a horse. You never forget how to do it. After studying the pair of poems, I make a number of observations.

BRAMBLES and THISTLES, mentioned in the long poem, grow around the wildlife pond. For its part THYME, mentioned in the short poem, may well survive in the former herb-garden. PETALS may stand for PETALSTON.

The word DUTY comes twice in the long poem, and once in the short poem.

Tony Fisher wears a blue velvet jacket. He may be the short poem's TROLL DRESSED IN BLUE.

In the course of performing her duty, Lady Beryl will put on CLOTHING that excites her LOATHING.

Miss Hegans has begun to repair a mandoline. She may be the short poem's LITHE LUTE-building GIRL.

Three questions sound in my mind, like the clear notes of a wooden flute, against the semibreves of Greta's deep steady breathing. Is the drivelling short poem organically related to the half-sensible long poem? Or is the short poem in some way born of the long poem? Do all the letters which compose the short poem come from the long poem?

I write out the larger cryptogram-square on a piece of white card.

Now comes the slow meticulous bit, which a real cryptanalyst always enjoys. In a whisper I spell out, one letter at a time, Lady Beryl's short poem. As I pronounce each letter I look for its twin on the white card, and cross it out. Experience warns me to expect that at some point I shall meet a letter in the short poem which has no counterpart in the long poem.

My expectation is not fulfilled. At length I realize that all one hundred and sixty-nine letters of the short poem have rôles in the long poem.

How many letters of the long poem have I not crossed out? One hundred and twenty? Better check the arithmetic. Yes! There are two hundred and eighty-nine letters in the long poem, and I have crossed out one hundred and sixty-nine of those letters.

Something moves me to write down, on a sheet of green paper, the one hundred and twenty letters of the long poem which I have *not* crossed out.

Hooohhh! Before my mental eyes, a thrilling notion begins to crystallize. I reach across the table, and pick up Tony's postcard. Lady Beryl's short poem contains the adjective CHILL. So does Mr Fisher's quatraine.

> *I have one black arrow under my belt,*
> *One for the grief that I have felt;*
> *That one is for Miss Greta Hegans,*
> *Whose chill disdain is my own chief grievance.*

How many letters does the black-arrow quatraine involve? One hundred and twenty. Have I inscribed each one of Tony's letters on my sheet of green paper? 'No!' cries a clever educated voice from the University of Lilliput. 'Don't be stupid.'

But the correct answer turns out to be YES. Four minutes later, having drawn one hundred and twenty strokes with my pen, I realize that the clever educated voice belongs to a conceited booby. Very good! The runes are read.

Near the door there hangs a blunt-horned ripping saw that really belongs in my workshop. Is it trying to yawn? Maybe I need fresh air! What should I do? Wake up Sleeping Beauty? No. The respiring body of my beautiful guest has united itself happily with a straight-backed wooden chair. I'll write her a note, and leave the shed in discreet fashion.

GRETA, DEAR, I'VE GONE OUT FOR A RUN, HAVING DISCOVERED THAT WHEN THE 169 LETTERS OF LADY BERYL'S SHORT POEM ARE TAKEN AWAY FROM HER LONG 289-LETTER POEM, THE 120 LETTERS OF TONY FISHER'S POSTCARD REMAIN.

Consider the case of an underslept man who has received a British classical education. Moonlight and a street-lamp can similize panoramas in that man's garden. For four seconds a shimmering Naiad, faintly resembliing Greta, favours me with a gelid scrutiny. Should I be in bed? Even Miss Poon and her telescope are at rest! An upstair light burns in the home of Mrs Herring, whose husband has been gravely ill for some time.

As I pass Delia's house, a line of the Chinese poet Du Fu comes into my head.

今 夕 復 何 夕

(What night can replicate the present night?) It is clear that Lady Beryl's 'cosmic quilt' is the temporal 'way' upon which she as 'author' travels. What modern counterpane will replicate the Petalston textual fabric? For a moment I think about the lattice structure of standard quantum logic. But hark! Words are riding on the wind.

'It is my duty to tell you, sir,' says the leaf-robed Naiad, 'that our interactive story will generate a great deal of foolish anger.' She smiles intrepidly. Then, in the cold air, her language takes on a geometric form.

```
I T I S M Y D U T
Y T O T E L L Y O
U S I R T H A T O
U R I N T E R A C
```

```
T I V E S T O R Y
W I L G E N E R
A T E A G R E A T
D E A L O F F O O
L I S H A N G E R
```

[The most sublimely cultured English, delivered in tones of complete assurance! 'Duty', not 'juty'. For some reason I think of the old valve radio -- made in 1938, housed in a large wooden cabinet, and still working – which lives in Delia's garden study. Whenever I listen to that radio, I hear the urbane self-confidence of a great empire. Like a crumhorn from the sixteenth century, every sonic instrument speaks in the voice of its own time.]

Crude and abominably loud, the radio of a passing car vomits out five syllables. 'Jean, she THREW her, she…..'

Physical exercise helps to preserve the sanity of thinking persons. I forget about everything, because a weary runner must concentrate on his course.

After fifteen minutes I come to Delia's church. Its electronic notice-board displays eleven words from Acts 16. 31. *Believe on the Lord Jesus Christ, and thou shalt be saved.* One minute later, a dissonant quartet of Christmas trees tries to make war on my happiness. It's funny. I like the innocent merriment of multicoloured lights, but in recent years four local gentlemen have elected to employ hi-tech monochrome scintillators. Alas! Their sterile tarantella of electric blue has turned one end of a happy street into a godless emotional necropolis. Our chilly gentlemen, all grandfathers, call themselves 'The Lads'. They could write a three-volume Encyclopedia of Mock Virility without any editorial assistance. In the days of their youth they sought *plaisir sans honneur*. Now, having reached the age of retirement, they sneer at every manifestation of good clean fun, like the Annual Water Fight which is run by Delia's church. The Lads have no real joy. Their bad-boy leers and guffaws are merely robotical. Dreading the eternal future, they roll the tongue of their memory around fusty dregs of rapture, much as bored children keep on tasting the two contiguous terminals of a nine-volt battery.

Course completed! And under the felt roof, Calypso is awake.

'Bravo, dear!' she says. 'Many thanks. I'd never have thought of doing what you've done, but your findings tally with the tale that I'm about to conclude.'

Without speaking I resume my seat. The shed is very warm.

'Yesterday morning,' Greta continues, 'I arrived in the art college at ten o'clock, annoyed by the idea that I had let Herdie down badly. I'll explain why in a moment.' She pauses. 'As I descended the stairway that leads to our ceramics department, I could hear Herdie talking to Cicely Grove – about the tremendous photograph of me which he had taken on the previous day. I was amazed. Filled with foreboding, I made my way into the kiln-room, where Cicely was making an enormous pair of bat-wings. "Hello, Greta!"

said a proud-looking Herdie. "Last night I developed your portrait, using coffee, vitamin C, washing soda, and ammonia." Solemnly he handed me this…..' Miss Hegans takes a picture from her valise, and sets it on the table. 'This low-tech latte. What do you think of it?'

Herdie's image does not belong to our world. It floats in temporal mist.

After ten seconds, a fatigued man makes his rather banal response. 'I don't recognize your face.'

'Of course you don't.' Greta speaks with the certainty of a logician. 'And there's no reason why you should. I mean, the picture doesn't look like me. It couldn't possibly look like me.'

'Why not?'

'Because…..' My visitor springs furiously to her feet, and shrieks out six syllables. 'BECAUSE I WASN'T THERE!' She stares at me for a while, and falls back on to her chair. 'Sorry, dear. I'll try to be rational.' Greta grimaces bravely. 'I spent two days of the holiday with my cousin Gillian in County Fermanagh. At eleven o'clock on the morning of the day before yesterday, I left Gillian's house in Maguiresbridge, allowing myself three hours to get back to Belfast and do a bit of shopping. After twenty minutes I came to a halt in a remote part of the country. No petrol! And by malign coincidence, I had left my mobile phone at home. I chose not to thumb a lift, reckoning that I might be picked up by a secret admirer of the Boston Strangler, so I walked, and walked, and walked. At a little after two o'clock I came to a petrol station. Here I bought and filled an emergency can. A farmer and his wife kindly drove me back to my car. When I reached the art college at four o'clock, and found it deserted, I phoned Herdie. He didn't answer. I drove home.' Greta pauses. 'Anyway! Between four thirty and ten thirty, I made twelve attempts to call Herdie, with the same result. I assumed that he was angry with me. But when I went into the kiln-room yesterday morning, I learned a devastating fact. Herdie believed that I had kept my appointment, and his belief was supported by photographic evidence.

'Then Cicely told me about Tony Fisher. About ninety minutes after Herdie took the photograph, Tony was found gibbering on the edge of our wildlife pond, with a longbow and a broken black arrow lying on the ground beside him. It was feared that he was suffering from exposure, so he was taken to hospital. Well! I was able to visit Tony at lunchtime yesterday. Although he had been delirious for most of the night, I found him quite lucid, transformed, and yearning to confess. He furnished me with what you might call the missing square of quilt.' Greta pauses. 'I was standing in the wildlife pond. As soon as Herdie left the scene, Tony emerged from cover, and prepared to kill me with an arrow. At once I vanished from the pond, and materialized beside him. When I compelled him, by the mere power of my will, to break his arrow in two, he realized that he was dealing with some preternaturally strong woman, and not with me. He fell on to his back. The woman looked at him kindly.

Speaking in what Tony called an incredibly aristocratic accent, she delivered a rhythmical incantation: "Greta will bring you her friend with a Bible." Three dactyls and a trochee. Early this morning, Tony wrote her words down on a paper towel. He gave me the towel before I left him. Look.' Miss Hegans produces a crumpled manuscript, and unfolds it carefully.

G	R	E	T	A	W
I	L	L	B	R	I
N	G	Y	O	U	H
E	R	F	R	I	E
N	D	W	I	T	H
A	B	I	B	L	E

'That is the story so far.' Lovely Calypso is utterly exhausted. 'I must go and lie down for four hours. You should do the same. But if you're free later in the day…..'

'I'll go to the hospital with you.'

'Thanks, dear.'

'Tell me one thing before you leave.'

'Shoot.'

'Do you hate the man who intended to murder you?'

'Do I…..' Greta regards me with the eyes of a fresh tiger. '*Hate* him? No!'

I get bathed and shaved. The desire for sleep has left me. After breakfast, having recalled the mild bright afternoon of 30 January, I paint a near-monochrome composite of Herdie's photograph, the Simpson miniature, and my own brief glimpse of a well-spoken Naiad.

There are many times in life when good work is fast work. After four hours, an altogether lovely person takes possession of the easel. That person is alive, and warm-blooded, but as remote from modernity as Lady Jane Grey. She has a formidable presence. (And of course my healthy living model is not the 'exact image' of her ancestress! If Greta is a gymnasium, Lady Beryl is an electric power station.)

May the spirit of a deceased human act, at the behest of its own will, *in the physical dimension*? II Samuel 12. 23 persuades me that it may not. But when a lady author lives a life of impeccable discipline, and when she works with great diligence to create a literary text, I believe in the power of her text. Any real writer who works hard enough will affect history.

Tony Fisher committed a physical act by breaking his arrow in two. Is it insane to imagine that the physical universe may be perfectly comprehended by the human intellect? Then many scientists are mad. ('There neither is nor can be anything which we are unable to understand. The only axiomatic universal constant is our all-surpassing human cleverness.')

'Never mind the human intellect,' a dull critic mutters, 'and forget about your nebulous irrational Naiad!' He sniffs. 'You have allowed yourself, in a moment of folly, to commit a very careless error. It is absurd to imagine that a real Victorian lady would use the modern word *interactive*.'

Who is this that darkeneth counsel by words without knowledge?

Here are two facts. Queen Victoria came to the throne in 1837, and the word *interactive* is lexically attested for the year 1832.

A third fact will demonstrate how rational the Naiad is. Her shapely language has begotten the title of our tale.

```
C O L L E C T E D V I S I O N S O F L A D Y B E R Y
L P E T A L S T O N T H E T O W E R I N S I L O A M
A S O N A T H R O N E A R E M O R B I D I L L S B I
D L A W N D E P O N E A W A R D E D W I L L S T H R
I V I N G B R A M B L E S F L O U R I S H N E A R T
H E S E V E R E D S T R E A M I W H O O N C E D I D
P E R I S H N O W C O M E B A C K I N D R E A M T H
O U G H M Y D I S T A N T D A U G H T E R M A Y N O
T H E A R M Y C R Y I W H O S E E T H E F U T U R E
W I L L N O T L E T H E R D I E G R E T A C A L L S
F O R B E R Y L T H I S T L E G R O W S A P A C E W
H E N Y O U S T A N D I N P E R I L I S H A L L T A
K E Y O U R P L A C E U N I M A G I N E D C L O T H
I N G C H A S T E L Y I E M P L O Y D U T Y Q U E L
L S M Y L O A T H I N G D U T Y G I V E S M E J O Y
```

```
A M I D S T Y O U R H E N R E S I D E S M Y C L U E
C H I L L C O D E D P E N T R O L L D R E S S E D I
N B L U E M A D U G L Y R H Y M E C O M E D U T Y G
O P A Y H U N G R Y T H Y M E T H E I R P E T A L S
K N O W W H A T L I T H E G I R L B U I L T M Y L U
T E P E A R L G R E Y J O I N C O S M I C Q U I L T
T H E A U T H O R S W A Y I T I S M Y D U T Y T O T
E L L Y O U S I R T H A T O U R I N T E R A C T I V
E S T O R Y W I L L G E N E R A T E A G R E A T D E
A L O F F O O L I S H A N G E R G R E T A W I L L B
R I N G Y O U H E R F R I E N D W I T H A B I B L E
```

But hark! Cicely Grove has come round to see me. Her tutor, one Reginald Dacke, has asked her to produce a compact piece of 'conceptual art'. Whatever Cicely creates must be based on a printed text. It must allude both to herself and to her tutor. It must also constitute a response to two 'key evil artworks' of which Dacke affects to disapprove: Gaston Bussière's *La Scène du Serpent*, and Agathon Léonard's *Femme Chauve-Souris*. By way of writing a 'propaedeutic narrative', Cicely's tutor has arranged eighty-five letters, with almost incredible cleverness, in five lines of seventeen. 'We wage war against key wickedness not by ignoring it,' Dacke has declared, 'but by confronting it.'

```
C I C E L Y G R O V E R E G I N A
L D D A C K E G A S T O N B U S S
I È R E L A S C È N E D U S E R P
E N T A G A T H O N L É O N A R D
F E M M E C H A U V E S O U R I S
```

What kind of tutor thrusts his own person into the work of a student?

After looking at the clock, I offer my visitor a lift to the bus station. She gladly accepts the offer. Three minutes later, I slow down and stop at a red light. For four seconds two seventy-year-old women regard me through narrowed eyes. Then they cross the road. Each woman is nearly six feet tall, and weighs about fifteen stone. Each one is dressed in very expensive but badly fitting clothes. Each one has short bleached hair. Each one wears heavy-framed plastic-and-metal spectacles. The woman on the left is carrying an accordion. The woman on the right is pushing an enormous grey pram, and I'm going to stop looking now, because unless I'm hallucinating the pram is occupied by a bonneted Alsatian dog.

Can things get any weirder? Oh, yes. When Greta and I meet for lunch, in an upstair café near the City Hall, we overhear two 'academics' conducting a conversation. Each one of these worthies radiates an insane self-importance, and for some reason they have both declared war on the English language. Instead of using words like 'main', or 'major', or 'vital', or 'important', or 'essential', they say KEY KEY KEY KEY KEY KEY KEY. And instead of saying 'some' or 'several', they say MULTIPLE, over and over again. Thirty per cent of their speech is booby-talk: 'cusp', 'raft', 'embeddedness', 'overarching', 'synergic', 'the target language', 'but that's a given', 'the silo', 'the descriptor', 'paradigm shift', some weird verb pronounced 'levveridge', and of course either 'diversity' or 'postcolonial' in every other sentence. Anything bad, undesirable or reprehensible is 'toxic', and every kind of idea is a 'narrative'. Seven times, I lie not, some supposedly naughty notion is described as 'a toxic narrative'. Oh, and every centre is an 'epicentre'!

After lunch Greta and I visit Tony Fisher in hospital. A mathematical fact may help you to remember a Biblical reference. The largest four-digit power of two is 8192, and the largest four-digit power of three is 6561. The difference between 8192 and 6561 is 1631. When Tony reads Acts 16. 31, he passes from darkness to light. Less than a minute later, a merry lady doctor comes in to tell her patient that he is free to go home. We offer Tony a lift.

'I feel like a limp aesthete,' says the grinning new creature. 'Will you please take me to a barber?'

Fourth tale: PILLOW-TALK

[A former member of the RCMP called Arthur Trench, who happens to be my cousin, works in an English university. He lectures in Russian, and runs the university's early music consort. Under his direction several students and a number of staff have recently begun to make early musical instruments. The group of new makers includes Charles Hartwell, who is professor of music. At the moment Arthur is talking to his wife Janet in bed.]

'I need to recruit more players, dear. Otherwise we're making instruments for no reason.' Arthur paused. 'I've been thinking. Last November you and I doubled the size of the fern-garden. Did we make a good job of it?'

'Yes.' Janet spoke in a puzzled tone. 'You know we did!'

'Well, then. Before long I'll have to double the size of the consort.'

'How will you do that?'

'Watch me! I mean, without boasting, love, I could get twenty new string players for the consort tomorrow. You wouldn't believe the number of yearning musicians who drop hints to me at the end of every concert.'

'Are they always string players?'

'No, not always. You get the occasional trumpeter, or trombonist, or bassoonist. Plus dozens of middle-aged recorder-players.' Arthur laughed. 'You have to be careful with *them*.'

'Why so?'

'Because unless they play something else as well, they tend to be absolute weirdoes. You know what I mean. Homeopathy, second-hand clothes, spectacle cords, tomato-plants in the bathroom, and a dusty four-year-old potpourri on every window-ledge. Recorder-players are *different*.' Arthur paused. 'You and I are quite normal. We're wearing pyjamas, and we're lying happily in a dark room. But recorder-players need more! They need knitted nightcaps, and cotton bedsocks, and the light of a Tibetan butter-lamp. Let me confess, dear. For *years* I've been wanting to send an article on recorder-players to a zoological journal.'

Janet laughed. 'You make them sound like members of a separate species.'

'That's what they are! So they're easy to identify.' Arthur inhaled luxuriantly. 'Recorder-players are all bespectacled from birth, softly-spoken, middle-aged, *even as teenagers*, and helplessly daft. Without being noticeably conceited, they believe themselves to be rather clever.' He paused. 'They would scare you, Janet. Listen! They're sitting beside you on a bus, and suddenly they start to eat *dried figs*. Their idea of a midday meal is a spoonful of cottage cheese on a lettuce leaf, a glass of freshly squeezed leek-juice, and a piece of raw garlic. Their idea of a mantelpiece ornament is either a dream-cudgel of driftwood, or a resin candlestick made in the form of Anubis. And they *never* dust their ornaments, let alone their books, which are either herbals, or horoscope manuals, or privately published anthologies of poetry by other recorder-players. They bath once a week. They wash their hair rarely, so as not to squander what they call "the natural oils". By the way, their instruments all smell of natural yoghurt. And their houses are always unheated, even in winter.' Janet remained silent, but the bed was shaking perceptibly. 'Their speech is a hideous stream of inconsequence. They never say "Yes" – it's always "Mmmmmmm!". They titter weakmindedly at everything. They insist on playing the recorder with their elbows up in the air. And they talk during rehearsals – either about some stupid "line-up of the planets", or about some new way of trisecting the angle.'

'What sort of music do they play?'

'Oh, their music is nearly always easy, and often trivial.' Arthur paused. 'Holborne's most vacuous piece, *The New Year's Gift*, is the *Eine Kleine Nachtmusik* of the recorder-playing classes. I mean, Janet, they genuinely *like* it. They prefer to perform music that they know well, so their repertoire is rather small. They play the same six or seven Dowland and Susato pavanes every month, always with the repeats – "*forte* the first time, and *piano* the second time" – even though the recorder has only one dynamic level. In between pavanes they gabble to their neighbours about the ghastly *communities* in which they mean to spend the second week of their Easter holidays.'

'What do they do there?'

'Oh, you know the sort of thing. Discovering your Inner Druid. Tantric nose-blowing. Unglazed pottery. Ephemeral art. Choral speaking with eurhythmics. Haitian folk-dancing. Gathering herbs by moonlight. How to use sheets of corrugated cardboard as extra bedclothes. Oh, and how to make cranberry cheese. Personal focus.' Arthur paused. 'The trouble is, they never focus on *anything*. Genuine focus would bring an end to their dabbling, dithering world of wooden beads, wind-chimes, kneeling-chairs, and Native American Wisdom.' He yawned exuberantly. 'You and I swam in the sea on every day of the Christmas holidays, Janet, and nobody knows. Recorder-players *paddle* for two minutes on a single day in August, and boast about it for weeks! You and I learn a lot from everything that we do, but they manage to learn very little, whether they're carving turnips or talking to cactuses. They doodle in the margins of life. Why? Because they've been born with an illimitable capacity for weak silliness.' Arthur yawned again. 'Everything about them is silly. I mean, they buy tins of ten-year-old talcum powder from sepulchral junk-shops. And *they all make candles* – if you don't make your own perfumed candles, you're not a recorder-player. They create barbaric pieces of para-jewellery from stainless steel blanks, tumbled pebbles, and resin adhesive. They squelch and squeak about in sandals whose soles are made from compressed peanut shells. The men wear ponchos, and yak-wool bonnets, and plus-fours. The women wear men's shirts, and cotton sou'westers, and no stockings on their DREADFUL legs. I don't know what you're laughing about, Janet Trench.'

'Arthur, where did you ever meet people like that?'

'Well, firstly in Canada, and then all over the world. I went to a recorder society for three years, when I was doing my first degree.'

'But do recorder-players all over the world conform to the same pattern?'

'Yes! Yes! Except in the Far East. And in Germany. And in the Netherlands. Elsewhere…..' Arthur exhaled like a whale. 'I've met recorder-players in at least a dozen different countries, dear. They're a breed! They can't help it. It's genetic – like being born a kleptomaniac. They *have* to play recorders.' The bed was shaking violently. 'They suffer from a genuine disorder. Like Münchhausen's Disorder, only scarier.'

'Arthur, dear, if you don't stop, I'm going to die.'

'Do you think I'm exaggerating?'

'Yes!'

'Well, I'm not.' Some unhappy dog whined in a neighbouring garden. 'I'm telling you, love, I can recognize recorder-players at a glance, the way you recognize other ballerinas. I see them in libraries, in auction-rooms, and in museums. They walk with *preternatural* inefficiency. They smile constantly, even when they're asleep. Oh, and they all wear bow ties and pocket-watches.'

'You wear a pocket-watch.'

'Be quiet. They *always* use recycled envelopes. They never weed their gardens. They weave scarves on tiny looms. They buy luxury editions of Culpeper and Gérard. They make dreadful patchwork quilts. And that's only the men. The women are worse. Female recorder-players have five areas of interest: vegetable dyes, natural birth, ginseng, garlic, and bran. They WORSHIP bran. They put bran in their unspeakable soups and curries.' Arthur paused. 'Last year an informer told me about the annual dinner of a certain recorder society. The dessert was a whipped syllabub containing flakes of bran. Janet, are you the source of that seismic vibration?'

At last Arthur's wife gave vent to her mirth. 'Waaaooohhhhh!'

'You'd think there was an aeroplane engine in the bed.'

'Waaaooohhhhh!'

'Will you please stop that outrageous noise, dear?'

'N-n-noooooo!'

'I'll get a bamboo, and beat you.'

'Ooooohhhh!'

'Behave yourself.' In truth, Arthur was glad to have a responsive audience. 'I wish I had you in my nine o'clock lectures, love. What was I talking about?'

'B-b-b-bran!'

'So I was. Listen, Janet. Recorder-playing women are *obsessed* with what they call "regularity", and they use bran as the Great Enabler.'

'Arthur, *stop it*!'

'They take bran and goat's milk for breakfast. They eat bran-and-oatmeal fritters instead of potatoes. And they make their own chipboard biscuits from bran, soya bean flour, and honey – a rare variety of honey, resembling asphalt, which may be legally purchased only by registered recorder-players. They drink elderflower water *voluntarily*.' Arthur paused. 'Whatever tea or coffee they give you at half-time always comes in big thick earthenware cups, and it's always "fair-trade", and it always sends the signal RUN-BABY-RUN to your bladder for the next two days, because it's always weak, and it's always cold. As its makers themselves are always pale. You *never* see a recorder-player with a tanned complexion. Because worst of all, male or female, they take no outdoor exercise. I've never yet met one of them who played football or hockey. That's why they need so much bran. Don't start me!'

'Well!' Janet wiped her eyes. 'I thought perhaps you had finished, dear.'

'I have.'

'Oooohhhhh.' Janet sat up, and leaned back against the studded leather headboard. 'Somewhere in your past, Arthur Trench, a number of recorder-players must have annoyed you rather badly.' She paused. 'Hartwell doesn't seem to like them either. In fact, now that I think of it, bits of what you were saying sound familiar! Last night Hartwell told me that he had been a *recorder tutor*. On a residential course.'

'Did he? He never told me that. What did he say about it?'

'Let me think. It took place during the last week of August. Hartwell said there were ninety people on the course. Sixty of them were good musicians, who played at least one orchestral instrument. *They* were all young. The other thirty were all middle-aged, very friendly, very loquacious, and completely useless – they could barely play their instruments, and they often sabotaged the ensembles that they tried to play in.' Suddenly Janet gave a little shriek of laughter. 'One of the middle-aged women believed that she had a Blue Aura! Hartwell said she was such an exponent of shameless flatulence that after two days he didn't merely believe in it – he *saw* it.' Downstairs the grandfather clock struck twice. 'Four of the women wore scarlet wellingtons, and two of them wore Dutch clogs.' Janet paused. 'One of the men, who wore a Nehru jacket, was always trying to burn incense in the dining-room.'

'Incense." Arthur sighed. 'Of course. I *know* those people.'

'Have you met them all?'

'No, no.' Arthur laughed. "Here's what I mean, dear. I haven't actually met any of them, but I could draw you what they looked like.'

'Oh, right. You mean you can discern their Lunatic Auras from afar.'

'Yes!' Arthur paused. 'Did Hartwell say anything else about them?'

'Well, he told me one fact that made me feel sorry for the staff.' Janet inhaled slowly. 'Most of the thirty oldies go round the same four or five courses every year, and so do their tutors! Hartwell said that his fellow-tutors were meeting the middle-aged brigade for the third time in two months.'

'I can hardly take it in.'

'What?'

'Hartwell having anything to do with a recorder course.'

'Oh, he told me why he did it. He had arranged some Bach organ music for recorders, and he wanted to hear what it sounded like.' Janet thought for a moment. 'It's funny. Hartwell mentioned ginseng as well, dear.'

'Did he really?'

'Yes! He said that some of the oldies took ginseng with their breakfast. And garlic!'

'There you are, then.' Arthur sat up. 'Now listen, Janet. You said *breakfast*.'

'So I did.'

'That word will lead us back to sanity. Do you want tea and toast?'

'Oh, yes.' Janet smiled in the dark. 'I really *love* you, Arthur.' She paused. "How did you know I was hungry?'

'Easy. I discerned your Gluttonous Aura. Wait here for five minutes, love, and then come downstairs.' Arthur got out of bed. 'Let me acquaint you with one arcane fact which no one *dares* to publish in an academic journal.' He switched on the light, went into the adjoining bathroom, and came out clad in his dressing-gown. 'When recorder-players decide to have a family, they put themselves on a diet which is five per cent by weight ginseng, and seven per cent by weight garlic.' Arthur paused. 'It's no wonder their children all look like Australian tree-ferns.'

Fifth tale: THE OLD PRETENDER

THEODORE Baldock, the elder son of humble parents, was an academic fantast.

After taking his degree he hovered around the university for six months, and worked as a part-time preacher. When he found employment in a local grammar school, he refused to cut the golden cord that connected him with high scholarship. Although Baldock was for thirty-eight years a conscientious teacher, inside and outside the classroom, he contrived to appear in the university's refectory every lunchtime, and in its library every night.

At the age of twenty-four, realizing that a belief in the Bible would win him few friends in the academic world, Baldock stopped believing in it. Two years later he joined a premier-league 'high' church whose choristers, archaically beruffed, nourished the spiritual side of his being. He felt that his weekly attendance at church conferred a genuine privilege upon the nebulous impersonal god in whom he now deigned to believe. It is a fact of life that Satan rewards his own followers before they die. In due time Baldock was asked to sit on the church vestry along with three professors, two lecturers, and the Esquire Bedell of the university. *My cup runneth over*, he told himself proudly.

The man was a successful and versatile bluffer. (Even his forename was a lie, for he had been christened *Thomas*.) He never taught sixth-form classes. He played no sport, but eventually became vice-president of the city's rugby and cricket clubs. On Saturdays he would appear at local pitches in order to shout insults at deficient players. He pretended to be an expert on Wordsworth. Although he was not a musician of any species, he would talk learnedly about sonata form to those who knew less than himself. He even sat on the committee of a local art-and-music festival along with Henry Poole, a music lecturer who was one of his best friends.

Baldock hated 'early' music, believing it to be primitive. He regarded *Eine kleine Nachtmusik* as the supreme achievement of European culture, and he listened indefatigably to certain popular classics. While he detested Bach, he loved John Rutter. Two of Poole's colleagues had never been introduced to Baldock. One was Charles Hartwell, the incisive professor of music. The other was Hartwell's friend Arthur Trench, a brutal dictator who ran the early music consort. Trench would have fled aghast from any member of the Baldock Collection ('A wandering minstrel I', 'Chorus of the Hebrew slaves', 'O silver moon', *'O mio babino caro'*, 'Songs my mother taught me', 'The Nuns' Chorus', and 'Take a pair of sparkling eyes').

Anyone who works in a university is acquainted by sight with an ambulant miscellany of human marginalia. Hartwell and Trench perceived Baldock dimly as a foolish man overwhelmed by the weight of his own importance. For his part the foolish man felt that Hartwell and Trench were threats to his very existence. It had horrified him to see

Arthur Trench wearing an I SHOT J.R. badge on the day of a carol service.

Theodore Baldock took the place of a mathematician. He regularly attacked what he called 'Hogbenism', imagined that Cartesian coordinates were first devised in a place called Cartois, believed that Tribonacci was an individual person, and had once pronounced 117 to be a prime number. His geography was a dream-world of confusion. He fancied that the two principal rivers of India were the Ganges and the Kamasutra. At the age of thirty-one Baldock had learned to distinguish Bologna from Boulogne, but he still equated Bratislava with Breslau, Lublin with Ljubljana, Potsdam with Poznan, and Vienna with Vienne. His history was little better: for example, he thought that Lord Novgorod the Great was an individual person, he associated Alfred the Great with Bannockburn, and he imagined that Cicero's wife was called Tully. What the exact difference was between Mascagni and Massanet, or between Metternich and Maeterlinck, the foolish man never learned.

Since the age of twenty-three Baldock had used the word *lamasery* to mean 'the hustle and bustle of a Lammas fair'. He reckoned that an Ovate received an ovation, that Fahrenheit was German for 'fire heat', and that *spindrift* was an alternative form of *spendthrift*. On one occasion he listened to a conversation between two lecturers from the English department. They were talking about Gerald Manley Hopkins. Baldock noted the word 'inscape', and deduced that certain poets were at pains to *escape into* their own verse. Two days later he overheard the professor of jurisprudence talking about 'letters of marque', and deduced that St Mark had written a number of epistles which for some reason were not represented in the New Testament.

Baldock made it a a matter of honour never to consult dictionaries or encyclopedias. He thought that *The Lusiads* were poems by Wordsworth. Whenever he heard Bazzini's *Ronde des Lutins* (= Dance of the Goblins), he was content to construe the French title as 'Round the Lupins'. One tiny cell of his mind, which was close to death from despair, knew that he was wrong in each case. A more capacious cell of Baldock's mind was home to a multitude of marvellous notions: Roderick Usher was an archbishop, David Lloyd George was the Welsh Rabbit, Sibelius liked tapioca, incunabula were night-demons, the scalene triangle was squamous, the Ember Weeks comprised the last four months of the year, Gingembre was January in the French revolutionary calendar, Cuspidor was one of the later months, Baudelaire had created the Fleur-de-Lis, Burnt Njál was a painter's pigment, Holofernes had something to do with the Holly Fern, George Eliot was the brother of T S Eliot, A E Housman was an English relation of Joris-Karl Huysmans, *corregidor* was Spanish for 'corridor', and there were exactly one hundred Chilterns.

Reckoning himself to be what Tennyson called a 'lord of language', Baldock judged the beauty and usefulness of an English word in accordance with one simple rule: bigger was better. Thus he perceived *contestation* to be better than *contest*, and *allegoresis* to be better than *allegory*. Sometimes, in the manner of the sorcerer's apprentice, he used a word without knowing its meaning. After eating a soft mint with his after-dinner coffee, for example, he would declare merrily, 'I am in a glorious state of *embonpoint*.'

Baldock qualified particular nouns with hackneyed adjectives: his explorers were 'intrepid', his Orientals were 'inscrutable', and his solicitors were 'desiccated'. He would insist on saying 'an historical novel', and then go on to speak of 'a hysterical reaction'. He always referred to Wales as 'the Principality'. He used three expressions – *inquorate, Lucasian*, and *of that ilk* – with insane frequency. He managed to mention either Tiglath Pileser or Antiochus Epiphanes every couple of days. And like hundreds of other halfwits, he described any medical man as 'the good doctor'. Although Baldock called himself both a classicist and a modern linguist, he could neither read a Horace ode, recite the Greek alphabet, crib his way through one page of a French novel, nor ask his way to the station in German. Some rogue had once told him, and he often repeated, that in Swahili *bang* meant a revolver, *bang-bang* a double-barrelled shotgun, and *bang-bang-bang-bang-bang-bang* a machine-gun.

Once a month Baldock posed in the library with a volume of Spanish literature, holding the book at a steep angle so that passing readers could see its title. In truth he disliked literature, and knew no Spanish, so he sublimated occasional words into clouds of fantastical gas, construing *enjoyar* (= to bejewel) as 'one who enjoys', and *orate* (= madman) as 'declaim'. One day, after ruminating the Santa Fe of black-and-white cowboy films, El Impostor told a credulous mechanic that the *auto de fe*, or *auto-da-fé*, was a vehicle invented by Wells Fargo. Baldock genuinely hated the professor of Spanish, who had more than once called him 'a wicked deceiver' to his face: but his hatred of France and America was a mere affectation.

On the afternoon of his twenty-eighth birthday, Baldock watched a very old and hilariously bad film about an English duke. Two weeks later the foolish man transformed himself into a lordly one. He taught himself to speak with eyes nearly closed, brows raised, and head held back. He cultivated a sing-song, slightly effeminate delivery, along with what he reckoned to be an upper-class drawl. He started to tell people, and soon came to believe, that he had been to Eton. If ever the chance arose he addressed a dog as 'sirrah'. When he found himself in the company of army officers he assumed an expression of awful solemnity, tightened his lips to the limit of possibility, and peppered his listeners with bullets of clipped speech. ('Bad case of Montezuma's Revenge,' one young major concluded.)

Baldock distorted three vowels hideously: after his niece Alva conducted her school band he would always say, *Elvaw's bend was ay heat*. By importunity and pertinacity he became in his own small world a kind of public speaker. Life is a funny business. While Baldock's grotesque accent persuaded his mostly stupid listeners to accept him as a fine orator, it also encouraged a few Connoisseurs of the Frightful to make, copy, and circulate clandestine recordings of his thirty-minute philippics. One mischievous lady even compiled a lexicon of Baldockian pronunciations: ell-èss

(= alas), ent (= aunt), bellay (= ballet), breetle, bress bend, creekeet, creeteek, deemweet, eeneveetablaaaayyyy (the final syllable of a full-dress Baldockian adverb always lasted for two seconds), een-tress-teeng, een-vee-jee-lay-teeng, greduallaaaayyyy, heenterlend, eell-weell (= ill-will), jeckess, jeckorendaw (= jacaranda), kempeeng, kerrots, leffeeng guess, Lett Een (= Latin), omeet, peenk, queff, queever, reedle, Spenneesh, theenkeeng, unmesked, vee-temm-eens, wreth, xen-thee-aw, yeah-hoos, zebraw, and many others including proper nouns like Eff-ree-caw, Frence, Mere-enn-daw, and Nedd-ee-aw.

Theodore Baldock automatically said about every political problem, 'No one seems to realize thet the whole metter eez quite seemple, and all one hess to do eez.....', even when the matter was not simple and there was no one thing that one might do. His own political notions – the sole relics of his upbringing – were devoid of complexity. Had they been put into practice, several thousand persons would have been hanged every week.

In a forty-minute retirement speech which ended with the words *Floreat Etona*, Baldock made a uniquely disgraceful exhibition of his own silliness, and promised to work full-time in the university. He kept the promise impeccably. He attended the funerals of staff and students. On Saturday he continued to abuse players of rugby and cricket for showing 'no kerrickter'. He devoted most of Sunday to his sister Ethel, who often said, 'Thomas has been a very good brother to me.' Every weekday he spent six hours in the library, and three in the refectory (an hour each for morning coffee, lunch, and afternoon tea). On Wednesday afternoon he allowed himself a thirty-minute stroll round the university grounds. On Thursday evening he attended a public lecture with his brother. On Friday night he fed a fierce lust in his forlorn bosom by studying a voluminous catalogue of academic costumes. On every single day of the exam season he worked morning and afternoon as an extra supervisor, loving the work, unlike the clergymen's wives and retired janitors who acted as his fellow-extras. Baldock was a sharp-eyed, assiduous, and humane supervisor. No sentry in time of war ever performed his duty more carefully. *Een ay veraay real sense*, he told himself, *I hev joined the uneeverseetaay steff.*

From its first matutinal period, the Elysian timetable of which Baldock had dreamed for decades ran its course without impediment, like the palace routine of a monarch restored. Within six months of his retirement the old pretender had become a fairly harmless piece of human furniture. Baldock was happy. Most of the students, and some of the staff, assumed that he was a retired professor. During his study hours he collected an assortment of bits and pieces, for he specialized in several different areas. Then, in his times of refreshment, he would often contrive to furnish a fellow-diner with some hot fact from the latest periodical. It was here that Baldock was noble, helpful, and good. But he was a bluffer in essence, and so he could be dangerous. If you spoke to him about a writer, composer, or painter of whom he had never heard, and sought his opinion, he would cannibalize any such information as came from yourself, and skilfully blend it in his answer with a credible fiction of his own. At his worst, he really was a wicked deceiver.

Baldock employed a number of devices to intimidate the simple-minded. One of his more successful tricks deserves to be recorded. First, he would attack a diligent scholar called, let us say, Oscar Otwell. He would go on to suggest – merely by referring with lofty contempt to 'Otwellism' – that Otwell had given his name to a pitiably facile doctrine. Then he would attack Otwellism as 'ay superfeecial darling of the Workers' Educational Essociation'. (If Baldock was talking about literature, he would pick on Arthur Waley. If he was talking about music, he would pick on Annie Warburton. If he was talking about art, he would pick on Aby Warburg.) By denouncing 'Waleyism', 'Warburtonism', and 'Warburgism', Baldock wantonly led his listeners to avoid a number of useful books. Being a man who worked hard only at his own image, he found it easy to insult a solidly excellent British institution. Like many another fantast, Baldock was a vulgar snob. He felt no shame in his working-class origins, for the sublime reason that he had long ago ceased to believe in them.

Today Baldock was taking tea with his friend Henry Poole in the refectory. Having received bad news from a publisher, Poole looked as if he wanted to cry. In spite of his misfortune, or perhaps because of it, the forty-year-old Poole appeared to have shed two decades. He made Baldock think of a captain dropped from the school team on the eve of a final.

'It would have been my first book, Theodore. Hartwell has written four books, and Trench has written three, but I've never wanted to rush into print.'

'No. I hev always been effraid of thet. Ez Lord Pemmerston used to say, eet's easier to get *eento* preent then *out* of eet.' Baldock looked up. 'Oh, hello, Prof. Utamaro. I thoroughlaay enjoyed your article een *Mutande*. Eet's time for us to uneeversellize Dantay, eezn't eet?'

'Yes! Yes! Thank you! Thank you!' The professor of Italian passed by.

'If I send it somewhere else,' Poole resumed, 'the editors are bound to ask me who has seen it already. Then I'll be obliged to tell them, and they'll think there must be something wrong with it.'

Baldock felt in the upper left pocket of his waistcoat. 'Take theece card weeth you,' he said. 'One of the lesser-known uneeverseetaay presses. Perfectlaay respectable. They weell almost certainlaay publeesh you, but they may esk you for ay substantial subvention.'

'I suppose that's the best I can hope for now,' said Poole. 'Thanks, Theodore. I'm glad I came in here.' He pocketed the card, rose to his feet, and went out.

Baldock closed his eyes, gave a mysterious smile, and shook his head slowly from side to side. After a minute he decided to join Prof. N S P Vane, who was taking tea with a colleague only three tables away. The professor of philosophy was known in his own world as 'No Serious Publications', so Baldock and he were firm friends.

Sixth tale: TOTAL WAR

ARTHUR Trench was a very happy man.

Geriatrics United Football Club had been established some years before. The idea of the founder members was to allow really incompetent footballers, such as they all were, to play a proper match every week. One of their number was a headmaster, who provided them with a pitch and a pavilion. Another was a short-sighted doctor, who loved dressing up in black and pretending to be a referee. Every Saturday the club's 'A' side (red tops, black shorts) would take the field against its own 'B' side (black tops, red shorts). Each player had two kits. Membership of the different sides was determined by lot on the day of the match. In general the standard of play was outrageously bad: OGs were quite common, and the word 'offside' was unknown.

From time to time the club would play an away fixture against a 'Proper Team'. Its twelve-year record in serious matches of this class was not impressive: played 39, drew 5, lost 34. Nonetheless any team that played against the Geriatrics quickly came to respect them for their fearless ferocity. 'Boys, you play a real hard game,' said one limping enemy at the end of a fiercely fought match. 'You're a very physical team,' said another. More than once the Geriatrics had hospitalized a promising young player. As a local journalist observed, 'These men take no prisoners.'

At Hallowe'en, four years before, they had gone on their first ever tour. One enterprising member of the club, who happened to be an architect, sent off a printed letter to his city-dwelling friends all over the UK. 'The members of Geriatrics United Football Club intend to visit your city on one of the dates shown below. We invite you to put together a team of utterly incompetent footballers, and play us a match.' Four of the targeted cities took him at his word, and eventually the challengers found themselves booked up to play in Glasgow, Durham, Newcastle and Carlisle. Against the expectations of everyone, they drew one match and won the three others.

That first tour changed everything. Fifteen gentlemen, all of them under forty, applied to join the club. Then the Geriatrics took over a disused shed beside the school pitch where they played, and converted it into a barless clubhouse. They began to enjoy the respect of their families, colleagues, and friends. The biggest change that they noticed was at home. There were no more complaints about the washing of their kits. Four magic syllables – 'won 3, drew 1' – magically altered the minds of ladies who up until then had regarded their menfolk as deluded Quixotes. One night a group of wives stormed into the clubhouse. At their behest the Geriatrics reconstituted their association as Teign and Dart Football Club. The wives immediately established a hockey-playing Ladies Section, and elected as their first president a dentist whose hobby was heraldry. Before long The Secret Project was under way.

It started as a great joke. Over time it took on a notable gravity as the women organized various social events to raise money for 'Club Development'. How much the whole thing cost very few people knew: but six months after their first tour the renamed Geriatrics were presented with dark green blazers whose opulent badges had been made in the Far East. (The badge-motto, IAM SENIORES SED CRUDI, was adapted from *Aeneid* VI by Arthur Trench, who at twenty-three was the youngest of the original members.) Reckoning themselves to be armigerous, the *seniores* immediately commissioned a multitudinous array of club ties, scarves, cufflinks, key-fobs, and hand-painted wooden shields. TDFC memorabilia appeared in the windows of two local sports shops, much to the rage of a certain rugby club, and sold rather well.

There was no stopping the Geriatrics. After deciding to accept 'social members', they started up a monthly Supporters Night for the enjoyment of tea, sandwiches, buns, and old films. Someone gave them an ancient piano, so they formed a choir. Then, being aware of their new dignity, they panelled the clubhouse entrance hall with oak plywood, and displayed their fantastical blazon of arms in a glass case on one side. 'You ought to have a trophies cabinet on the other side,' the dentist said wistfully. She was overheard by a club member who taught technology. That man said nothing, but he worked for four months in his spare time to give the club both a worthy cabinet, and a worthy trophy (the Steel Cup, made of riveted two-inch-by-half-inch steel rectangles). He presented the cup to great acclamation at the club's first proper AGM. Those present voted to establish an annual competition in which the 'A' team would play the 'B' team for the Steel Cup at some point between Christmas Day and New Year's Eve.

As it turned out, the competition might better have been held at another time. Several players would be away over Christmas, several would be entertaining visitors, and others would be out of action by reason of indulgence. Thus it happened that a university lecturer called Arthur Trench played in the Steel Cup Match every year. He was always back at his family home for Christmas, he was an utterly useless footballer, he paid his dues and wore the club blazer, so he was an obvious person to ask.

Today he was happy to be playing right back for the 'B' side. At nine o'clock he and his wife had swum to the harbour mouth, and then run home. ('The soul of my dear husband rejoices,' Janet often said, 'in *severe disciplines.*') Yet severe discipline was not the only source of Arthur's present happiness. He was looking forward to a late breakfast. He felt wonderfully at ease with the idea of two twenty-minute halves. Furthermore, at thirty-one he was the second youngest man on the pitch. Ten of the other players looked as if they had discharged themselves from hospital an hour before. There was one enormously tall customer on the 'A' side whom he had been warned about. ('Watch that big boy Charlie, Arthur, he plays for the 'B' side of a Proper Team.') But presently, six minutes into the first half, the big boy didn't seem to be much of a threat. Like Arthur, he hadn't had a touch of the ball yet. Charlie was standing in the middle of the park, doing something to his bleached hair with three inches of broken comb. Arthur smiled grimly. Not much to worry about there. And then –

'Get back and defend!' the 'B' keeper was yelling.

The comb had disappeared, and Bleach Boy was in possession of the ball. He was coming down towards the goal like a killer whale, with four of Arthur's team-mates gasping uselessly behind him. In a moment he would shoot. There was only one thing to do. Arthur ran straight into him, hard. The ball wandered off harmlessly to the right.

'Refer*ee*!' Bleach Boy was lying there like the Dying Swan. Arthur held out a hand and helped the fallen hero to his feet. Had that been a foul?

'Play on,' said the man in black

Arthur relaxed. The doctor wasn't taking any nonsense.

'That fellow's an evil animal,' said a lady spectator.

'Do you really think so?' asked Janet in a frigid voice.

'I really do.' The lady was silent for a while. 'Is he your husband?'

'Yes, he is!'

'I'm sorry. The other man's mine.'

Charlie took his revenge by scoring two exhibition goals before the end of the first half. All the spectators applauded him in a fair-minded spirit. But when Bleach Boy knocked in a contemptuous back-heeler in the middle of the second half, and saluted his own brilliance with a coarse guffaw, not everyone was amused.

'Worse than bestial,' muttered that paragon of local gentility, the doctor's wife.

Janet wondered if all was lost, but for the last ten minutes of play the 'B's fought back against a three-goal lead, and showed what they were made of. Two lucky crosses, both majestically put away by a forty-year old bus-driver, were in due time followed by an OG from the 'A' left back, and the score was even with less than two minutes on the clock.

The 'A's seemed to be collapsing. Apart from Bleach Boy they all looked desperately ill, and they were allowing five members of the 'B' side to congregate not far away from the 'A' goal-mouth. Arthur Trench was up there with the hopeful squad, enjoying fantasies of glory.

Suddenly it all went wrong. The 'A' captain moved backwards to take a header, and knocked over the referee. The bus-driver from Arthur's team took possession almost by accident. For no reason he passed the ball to Bleach Boy, who began to walk languidly up the left of an almost empty field.

'Get back! Get back!' the 'B' keeper cried out in anguish.

One of the 'A' midfielders, a lay reader from Arthur's home church, started to run up on the right to take the cross.

Arthur trotted up the field after Bleach Boy, who had begun to walk briskly.

Then, as the referee was putting on his glasses, there was a most appalling piece of play. The bus-driver, trying to make amends, hurtled off to the right at amazing speed. He overtook the 'A' player who was running to take the cross from Bleach Boy, and brought him brutally to the ground in a manoeuvre which he would later describe as 'the flying crowbar'.

The referee looked at his watch. 'Play on!' he said, but for a few seconds the game appeared to have stopped.

Bleach Boy had paused in his course. With upheld hands he implored heaven to witness.

For some reason no member of the 'A' team was eager to replace the bus-driver's victim.

'Don't worry, boys, Charlie has it in the bag now,' said the 'A' left back. Action resumed.

Flying Crowbar moved slowly across the pitch towards Bleach Boy, who had begun to run.

'Go right of him, Arthur!' the 'B' keeper called.

Arthur obeyed, and ran in a great arc.

Some men would have tried to go for the ball, but not Arthur Trench.

He knew his limitations.

He refused to endanger his own team by committing a Little-Boy-Blue act of theoretical rectitude.

Above all, he believed in the Geriatric policy of total war.

So once he had overtaken his quarry, he turned suddenly and charged right into him, hard.

Bleach Boy crashed to the ground with a moan of impotent fury.

The ball trickled away slowly.

'REFEREE!' screamed the woman who was standing beside Janet.

The doctor favoured his interlocutrix with a friendly wave. 'Play on!' he said.

Flying Crowbar sent the ball into enemy territory with a classical toe-pointer.

Ten seconds later the 'A' right back shouted, 'Keeper!', and headed in the second OG of the match. Three blasts on the whistle sounded for full time. Bleach Boy was helped to his feet. The 'B's had won the Steel Cup.

What followed bore witness to the essential goodness of the players.

The two teams clapped and cheered each other.

The captain of the 'A' team presented the Steel Cup to the captain of the 'B' team.

Everyone applauded, and cameras were produced.

Flying Crowbar was photographed with his victim. ('My cousin,' he explained proudly.)

Bleach Boy thumped Arthur on the back, and said that he always respected a dedicated killer.

Then the twenty-two footballers shook hands with each other. They even shook hands with the referee.

Farewells were exchanged, and ladies came up to claim their menfolk.

'Well played, big boy.' Janet took her husband's arm. 'Now listen. There's a woman over here who wants to murder you. Come this way, dear, and do your best to calm her down.'

Seven minutes later Arthur, Janet, and the two Bleaches were sitting at the only outdoor table of a well-known café, whose proprietor hailed from Belfast. Members of both 'A' and 'B' teams smiled as they walked past the café with their consorts. Three children raced along the roadway on their new tricycles. A boxer and a Labrador led their owners over to the cafe, and sniffed at Janet's ankles. Both dogs were immaculately groomed. The sun shone with all his might. A glorious harmony reigned. Charlie was talking to Arthur about a local church. His wife Brenda was talking to Janet about the Brandenburg Concertos.

Laughter came from the kitchen, where four Full-Size Cooked Breakfasts were being prepared. Each diner would soon have to deal with two pieces of bacon, two steak sausages, two eggs fried hard, two pieces of soda bread, two pieces of potato bread, plus generous quantities of mushrooms, tomatoes, and baked beans.

Arthur Trench was a very happy man.

Seventh tale: I WANT CLOTHES

'WHAT we see is often a combination of what we want or expect to see, what we think we ought to be seeing, and what we have seen in the past.....

'We clothe images of the unknown in the garments of the known. Thus the word "alien" suggests some kind of articulate biped. Thus four meaningless marks on a little patch of wallpaper combine to suggest two eyes, a nose, and a mouth.....

'We see menacing things in the dark because we carry the tropes of menace in the dark part of our own minds.....

'Sometimes the tedium of normal existence leads us to enter some kind of artificial labyrinth. We ride on ghost trains, and we watch horror films.....

'The memory of any visual experience may be weakened by contemplation, or by the passage of time.....

'Human beings have free will, so Macbeth is under no compulsion to act in accordance with what the witches say.....'

It was Monday morning, and Stephanie Owen was sitting in her English class. Instead of listening to the bearded Mr Faughan, she was reading a popular journal of psychology.

The earnest boy who sat beside Stephanie reckoned that she had chosen to live rather dangerously.

NADRAT, the National Association of Drama Teachers, had arranged a weekend conference that would be talked about for years to come. Friday night was taken up in standard fashion with a brief AGM and a lavish dinner. Saturday morning and afternoon were filled with the customary lectures and presentations. Saturday night was different. Instead of the usual drinks party in a Cambridge hotel, there were two pieces of real drama. At nine o'clock the poet Daniel Burnham presented his own minimalist version of Milton's *Comus*. By way of prelude, the Italian actor Roderigo Maschera intoned a thirty-minute soliloquy against a background of sturdy chordal music. Maschera drew his text, according to the programme note, from Francesco Colonna's *Hypnerotomachia*, of which no member of NADRAT had ever heard. His soliloquy was accompanied by sixteen recorder-playing Dryads whose two-piece swimsuits were made of plastic ivy-leaves.

These Dryads were the leading ladies of their school dramatic societies, and they had been selected during the Christmas holidays on the basis of six criteria: they were all of 'outstanding personal appearance', they were all at least five feet ten inches in height, they were all physically fit sportswomen, they were all accomplished players of an orchestral woodwind instrument, they were all accomplished players of the tenor recorder, and they were all eighteen years old. The Dryads were brought to the conference by their drama teachers. Three of them came from Scotland, two came from Northern Ireland, and one came from Wales. Ten others came from various parts of England. During the whole of the previous night, all sixteen Dryads had been unable to sleep. They were excited for five reasons. They would be far away from their own schools. They would be acting in a real drama. They would have the chance to make contacts that might be important for their future dramatic careers. They would be able to make a lot of interesting new friends. Above all, their little play was going to be recorded for Italian television.

After the Friday dinner, Maschera rehearsed with his accompanists for four hours. He impressed them by speaking in impeccable British English. First of all he taught them how to stand – not like marble pillars under pressure, but like steel piano-strings under tension. Then he taught them how to suppress coughs, sneezes, and yawns. It delighted the Dryads to discover that their preceptor had no interest in the suppression of laughter. As a director Maschera was at once demanding, and gentle, and hilarious. While he addressed his troupe of Dryads as 'darlings', he never failed to address an individual actress by name. Before the end of the evening rehearsal, each of the girls came to feel that she had known her director for several years.

'When I listen to you,' Maschera said, 'I hear superb musicians who have practised their parts diligently. When I look at you, I see heart-stopping young women of immaculate beauty. You are made of human flesh, and you have red blood in your veins. I should love you all to join me for a six-month camping holiday in Sardinia, but alas! – the local *banditti* would cut my throat, and sell you to the Turks, so we shall allow that delectable vision to fade away.' He paused. 'It pains me to tell you, my darlings, that at present your flesh-and-blood selves are of no earthly use to me. I need you to convert yourselves into entrancing vegetal creatures who derive their nourishment from soil and water. In fact, I need you to become alluringly cold beings who have green sap in their veins.' He paused. 'How may all of you undergo such a conversion?'

'We use our imaginations,' ventured the Welsh girl.

'Yes, of course, Stephanie, you use your imaginations. Very good, darling!' Maschera beamed. 'But that will not be enough. Conversion, you see, is a volitional thing. You must all *desire* to become Dryads. You must turn yourself into Dryads by a conscious effort of the *will*. And once you have succeeded in *becoming* Dryads, you must concentrate religiously, with every cell of your being, on *remaining* Dryads.' He paused. 'From now on, do your best to think like trees. Think of feeding in terms of sucking up nourishment through your roots. Think of clothing in terms of ivy-leaves, and try to wear your costumes for as much of the next twenty hours as you can. Think of *home* as the physical tree in which you as a spirit reside. Think of friendship solely in terms of your fellow-Dryads. Think of romance purely in terms of the wind that plays around your body by night. Forbid yourselves to long for any species of humanish otherness. Some of you have boyfriends.' Maschera regarded his pupils sternly. 'Promise me, my darlings, that you will forget about those incredibly fortunate gentlemen until our little play is over. Promise me also that you will cease to remember the mythological clichés that you have picked up in the course of your education. Refuse to entertain any pulse-quickening thought of being pursued by the formidable god Faunus. Expel from your minds any yearning for an encounter with voracious goat-leggèd satyrs.'

Four of the English girls laughed nervously.

Maschera grinned like a bucolic schoolboy, and continued. 'Try to conceive of yourselves as being related to tangible features of the natural landscape: grass, nettles, primroses, wood sorrel, brambles, ferns, mosses, bushes, trees, stones, different kinds of soil, plus the water of ponds, lakes, streams, and rivers. Drink into yourselves the actual *spirit* of these physical things.' Maschera flexed his arms, clenched his fists, and inhaled theatrically. 'I have nearly done! Mark me well, my darlings. Tomorrow night, at the climax of an otherwise plain-clothes version of *Comus*, you will see an all-green Sabrina dressed in garments very like your own. The colour of that lady's skin will make her audience gasp. Do I want *your* audience to gasp? Yes, of course! Why then do I not ask you to wear an all-green make-up? Because I want your greenness to come *from within you*. I want you to *radiate* greenness. If you give me what I want, the audience will believe that you are green on the outside as well as on the inside. Remember! Real acting is not about wearing make-up and costumes. Real acting is about compelling an audience to see you as you choose to be seen. Any one of you who learns that simple lesson will be able to convince her English teacher on Monday morning that he is looking at an ivy-clad Dryad.' Maschera blended panic with amusement in a most sophisticated grimace. 'That's enough talk from me about acting! I don't want to tire you, my darlings. Please go and retrieve your instruments from the table at the back. By the way, I promise to have those ludicrously American poinsettias removed before tomorrow night.'

When the girls returned, Maschera continued. 'Look at your instrument. Apart from its cedar block, it is made from a single piece of hornbeam. It is plainly cylindrical on the outside, with no fancy turning. It has an unusually wide cylindrical bore. It has a range of only a ninth. Its optimal sound is strong, elemental, woody, and uncompromising. Let me repeat some of the instructions that you received months ago with your instrument. If you want to produce the proper sound, you must employ all the resources of your body. Breathe in through your mouth with brash confidence. Fill your lungs to their limit. Then blow as hard as you can without letting the notes go out of tune. Let a steady stream of air pour from the bottom of your lungs to the beak of the instrument. Hold nothing back. And don't forget to stand tautly! Remember to pull in your stomach as you play.' He paused. 'Your recorder represents your tree. You love your recorder, because you love your own tree. Let your affection for your instrument come out in the music. Develop an affection for your recorder during tomorrow's rehearsals.

And tonight, develop a staunch affection for your fellow-Dryads. How may you do that? I'll tell you. Don't go to bed! You know how to act, and you know how to play your instruments, but you don't know each other. You are still sixteen individuals. You are not yet members of a genuine ensemble. Well, then! Go for a five-hour walk. Keep to the main roads. Talk continually. Don't talk to any one Dryad for more than twenty minutes. Study all fifteen of your colleagues carefully. When you get back to base, wash yourselves in freezing cold water. Eat as little as you can for breakfast, and be content to eat only a little fruit for the rest of the day. There will be a gargantuan supper at the end of the evening. You can fall upon that supper like the harpies in canto 13 of Dante's *Inferno*. Until then, allow yourselves to suffer deprivation. Alas! I must suffer deprivation myself. Every night, when I am working at home in Turin, I drink three cups of peppermint tea, but the merciless Eumenides who administer the kitchen belowstairs are unable to supply me with any such elixir. We suffer together, my darlings.'

Stephanie looked at her producer thoughtfully. She had grown up on a farm near Aberystwyth. Until the age of sixteen she had loved everything to do with plants. When people asked her what she hoped to study at university, she would reply, 'Horticulture.' After taking part in her first school play, she turned into a different person, and resolved to become an actress. For the last two years she had felt little interest in the natural world. Maschera's mention of peppermint tea led Stephanie suddenly to think about old beloved things. She considered plants, and places. While the drama teachers were staying in an expensive hotel, their star pupils had to live like Spartans in an outdoor resource centre. Beside the centre was a little forest which all sixteen girls had explored on the afternoon of their arrival. Stephanie wondered if she might be able to find watermint growing beside a stream in the forest.

But Maschera was addressing her. 'Miss Owen, you were brave enough to answer my first question tonight, so I appoint you Archdryad. It is exactly 2 am. Tomorrow we rehearse for seven hours. Look after your colleagues!'

Twenty-four hours had passed, and everything had gone well for the Dryads. Strange to relate, the little Italian drama completely ravished an audience which understood not a word of Maschera's soliloquy. (Nearly everyone pronounced the slender-limbed Dryads to be 'ethereal'!) Having been honoured with a standing ovation, the Ethereal Ones decided to enjoy Milton's *Comus* as front-row spectators. A sensation was created by the all-green and very tall actress called Tamara Wells who starred as Sabrina. Before she sang her song, Tamara played its four-note melody on a conch which had been pierced with three fingerholes. Miss Wells was an actress of rare beauty. She sang like Echo, and played her shell-trumpet like a full-time Tritoness. While the applause for *Comus* was dying away, a lady fire-eater of astounding pulchritude came on as a surprise item. This ill-starred maiden turned out to be a damp squib, because some clever boy left all the house lights on. Finally, at ten thirty, a

Babylonish feast of vol-au-vents, pizza slices, egg-and-cress sandwiches, tiny meat pies, oatcakes with mackerel pâté, cheese straws, pineapple creams, toffee-and-banana tarts, little syrup puddings with custard, ice cream, and hot tea was served to all comers. The sixteen girls managed to wolf twenty per cent of the available foodstuffs. People continued to marvel at the loveliness of the Dryads, but after a few minutes they stopped using the word *ethereal*.

Now the sixteen girls were back where they really belonged. They had been in uproarious form since they left their austere dormitory through its only window. Once they reached the forest, they became less noisy. A friendly moon was shining with all her might upon the well-worn path that led through the forest. What were the young actresses doing? They were enjoying an Arcadian adventure. The idea of staying awake for a third night was due to Stephanie, who was furtively carrying a small bottle. Miss Owen had declared that the place for costumed Dryads was a wood, not a dormitory.

Avidly the girls savoured the freshness of the air, and the smells of the forest. They tripped over briars, they were stung by nettles, and they cut the soles of their feet on stones, but they saw these discomforts as worse than trivial. Every so often the Archdryad made them all run on the spot and beat the air for two minutes. At a little before two o'clock – only Stephanie wore a watch – the girls came to the bank of a tiny lake, and sat down on a carpet of dried pine needles. They began to talk about the all-green Sabrina, about the fire-eater, and about Daniel Burnham, the producer of

Comus. All of them liked Burnham, whom they regarded as an important contact. He had treated them with exceptional friendliness. Fifteen of them liked Sabrina. (The exception was a Glaswegian girl called Victoria, who thought that Tamara Wells was a self-idolater.) Eleven of them agreed that they had never seen a more wonderful beauty than the fire-eater, a well-known young model called Angela Delvigne. All of them felt sincere affection for Roderigo Maschera.

'Do you know what?' It was Victoria who spoke. 'I don't want to be the sublime Tamara Wells in an all-green make-up, and I don't want to be the divine Angela Delvigne in a two-piece swimsuit of studded scarlet oxhide. I'm glad to be myself.' She paused. 'You girls should be glad to be yourselves. Every one of us attracted a lot of attention tonight. We're different from each other, but we're all very beautiful. Probably more so now than we ever will be.'

'What do you mean?' Stephanie asked.

'I mean we've reached our peak,' said Victoria. 'We'll never look any better than we do now. Oh, I may grow out a bit here and there, but I'll never have a better waist than my present one.' She yawned. 'I don't want to get any older.'

With a sense that people were feeling embarrassed, Stephanie looked at her watch. 'Listen, you nymphs,' she said. 'We stayed awake all last night, and now we're in danger of going asleep.' She rose to her feet. 'Stand up and follow me without making a sound. Don't squeal. Remember you're a Dryad.' She paused. 'We're going into the lake. Stay in for as long as you can. Once you come out, you can walk around the forest on your own. Try to keep away from everyone else. At five o'clock I'll come back to the lake and start singing. Follow the sound, and we'll all meet back here.'

Stephanie's fifteen colleagues followed her obediently into the lake, which was more than deep enough to swim in. Although the water was cold, no one made any sound of complaint. All the girls were revelling in the power of a new experience. *It's vital to do the sort of thing that we're doing now*, they thought, and of course they were right, because they were bright. Rectitude has little to do with languid conventional dullness. So long as their conduct neither harms themselves nor disturbs others, bright people should never be fettered by the expectations of the dull. A bright student may learn as much by staying out all night, for some curious purpose, as by sitting at a desk for the thirty hours of a school week. One-eyed preachers of the *early-to-bed* doctrine offer us an expurgated universe with no bats, no night-scented stock, and no stars.

The girls drank in greedily every element of the drama which enfolded them. (A moonlit lake, surrounded by tall trees. The discreet plashing of water. Fifteen new friends.) No one laughed or spoke. Here was a play which might be enjoyed only by those who enacted it. Each of the sixteen performers had experienced far too much in terms of only two senses, through the medium of television, and not enough in terms of all five. Tonight was real. It was therefore so unusual that everyone felt enthused. *People who sit in a warm room*, Stephanie thought, *can* contain *the two-dimensional experience that is brought to them by a flat screen.* (The screen may be smaller than the seat of a chair!) Sometimes watchers of television have to tolerate the absurdity of huge expanded faces, but more often they encounter things that are much smaller than themselves – things with no smell, no taste, no temperature, and no tactile quality. Even televisual darkness is a cheat. By contrast, you can't contain a path, or brambles, or a flying bat. These things are external to yourself. The path addresses the soles of your feet. The brambles catch at your ankles. The flying bat encourages your eyes to range over a broad vista.

Then you achieve intimacy with the lake by immersion. You surrender yourself to what surrounds you. The water has a mysterious quality. As you swim, its caressing liquidity massages away the wounds of stone and thorn.

While the cold water banished all weariness, it heightened the perceptive faculties of sixteen girls who had gone without sleep for a long time. No one complained, even in her own mind. *I'm not proving how hard I am to my fifteen friends*, each girl thought. *I'm proving it to myself.* It was eight minutes before the first swimmer came out, and fifteen minutes before the Archdryad left the water.

Stephanie smiled to herself. She felt good. (When you got out of an indoor swimming pool, the air seemed to be cold! Here, tonight, it was the other way round.) She combed her long wet hair vigorously with eight fingers. Soon she could feel it hanging around her face in an untangled state. Now for an experiment. Where was her bottle? There it was! Lying at the root of a rowan-tree, with a demure troop of late-blooming primroses to guard it.

Stephanie opened the bottle. It was strangely pleasurable even to inhale the vapour.

The medicinal virtues of the liquor were apparent in its dominant overtones – almost like the smell of whatever it was – ether? – in a hospital ward. Mr Faughan often declared that peat was a major part of the bouquet of good quality malt, but he was merely repeating a commonplace. To Stephanie, the top notes suggested a heap of well-fermented compost, freshly disturbed after a period of heavy rain. Intriguing stuff? Oh, yes! Especially when the damp warmth of the initial pungency gave way to subtle and complex undercurrents.

Stephanie smiled again. She could stand and inhale until sunrise, like a beetroot-faced connoisseur swilling VSOP Cognac about in a great balloon, but the only way to explore the elusive, half-perceived landscape of the flavour was to taste the actual fluid.

Stephanie had never drunk any spirit before.

She put the bottle to her lips.

The whiskey was hot in her mouth.

After a moment her oesophagus and her stomach were lit up with a warm enriching glow. Then her mouth asserted its primacy, and there the spiritous sensation gave way to a group of almost indefinable tastes. Porridge. The past. A metallic tongue-twang-tang which she linked at once with her cousin's train set: electric, and unmistakeably blue in colour.

Another mouthful. Yes! Without doubt electric. And something else as well: earthy, organic, almost meaty, like rare steak, or like recently turned soil. Persistent, and weirdly compelling – it was neither 'nice', nor so strange as to be unpalatable. In fact, the whiskey had a flavour that made you want to take another swig, so that you could see if it really did taste like that.

Stephanie finished the bottle, capped it, and pushed it into a patch of soft, yielding soil between two fern-roots. She realized with surprise that the liquor was already working on her faculties. For a moment the tall girl was affected by a genial kind of whooziness. She felt as if she wanted to lie down on the pine needles. Then she experienced a bizarre sensation. It was as if she had been driving too fast in the dark, and arrived suddenly at an unexpected dip in the road. At once the thought of sleep left her mind. Ten feet away, the trunk of a mature pine stood up inscrutable in the moonlight. Stephanie walked over to the tree, and kissed it gravely. That satisfied her not at all, so she embraced its scaly bark with her arms and thighs. As if in response, the pine began to engulf her with its tonic breath, evoking a memory from her human past. One day Stephanie's divinity teacher had taken his whole class outside, and made each student embrace a particular tree. 'Get to know your own tree,' he had said. 'Every tree is a child of the universe, like yourself.' Stephanie had laughed out loud on that day. Tonight, as she wrapped herself around the silent, breathing giant, she was filled with devout joy. *I love you*, she thought.

A breeze arose, and played on her back. *I love you*, it seemed to say. *You are supremely beautiful. Don't be too sober. Dance with me.*

Stephanie shivered not with cold, but with an almost timorous delight.

Incongruous and simple, there came into her mind a poem from one of the first books that she had ever read.

> Oh, Wind, you're very rough today,
> You blow the clouds along,
> You puff my chimney smoke away
> And sing a windy song.
> You shake the washing to and fro,
> You make me dance and sing,
> You take my little bell and blow
> To make it jingle-jing!
> Jingle-jingle-jingle-jing!
> Oh, it is a happy thing
> To have a little bell to ring!

After kissing the bark of her tree for a second time, she walked back to the grassy lakeside. In her mind there sounded not a little bell, but a sopranino saxophone made of boxwood. Wildly, willingly, empowered by the music and its player, she began to dance around the lake. Her partner was the wind.

How long a time she spent in dancing Stephanie did not know. When at length she found herself wrapped around the tree once more, gasping for breath, she looked at her watch. Nearly three o'clock! Time was moving swiftly. The young Dryad was warm, dry, and pulsing with life.

She lay down intrepidly on a gravelly patch of ground near the bank of the lake, and reached out at a venture with two long arms. Her right hand happened to touch a large dockenleaf. Stephanie pulled the cool leaf from its stem, and held it to her brow. For a few minutes she considered the marvellous theatrical events of the last two days. Everything had gone really well. Were all the other Dryads engaged in a similar kind of review?

Maybe not. Who could tell? Perhaps they were thinking normal, well-behaved, good-girl thoughts about going back to the dormitory, and turning in! Such thoughts did not appeal to Stephanie. How could she go back to the dormitory, and turn in, and go to sleep, and do nothing? It didn't matter that she had no great list of important things to do. The moon was shining. That fact in itself made being out here better than going to bed and doing nothing. Tonight was not the sort of night for going to bed, Stephanie told herself.

She sat up slowly, and looked around. The shadows of trees and bushes were stark on the surface of the lake. Moonlight seemed to endow each particular shadow with a magical solidness. Now that the wind had died down, Stephanie realized that the night was rich in meaningful little noises. Most of these noises were softly percussive. They spoke of movement, and they came to her ears with the force of an oracle. The 'nocturnal animals' of a school textbook were silent as death on a page, but if you took the trouble to join them in their own appointed time, and if you opened your ears to the music of their world, you realized how busy these animals were. Once the sun rose, they would rest in silence. And once breakfast was over, Stephanie thought happily, she would instal herself in her teacher's little green car, wrap herself in his tartan rug, and sleep the whole way back to Aberystwyth. Oh, dear. Was her Dryadic persona already beginning to wilt?

No, it wasn't. That young-eyed persona was more alive than before, and it had grander things to contemplate than complacent human warmth. For the first time Stephanie became aware that the lake had both an inlet stream and an outlet stream. She found herself able to apprehend the contrapuntal music of two streams – the inlet mostly in her right ear, and the outlet mostly in her left. It astonished her to perceive how close she was to a music that had always been sounding. Every so often there was a sudden little solo-note of crystalline merriment, and her heart leapt.

At length, like a ballerina, the moon began to float majestically above Stephanie's pulsating new world. The

Dryad found herself able to see trees, and bushes, and the lake itself, clothed in a radiance that took away all the mystery and the terror of night. As she herself had exchanged a complicated school uniform for two brief garments of ivy, so the new world around her had laid aside the complexities of day, and arrayed itself in an almost transparent robe of silver. Could anything be more simple? Stephanie set herself to unite with every perceptible feature of the landscape. She did her best to harmonize with beings whom she now saw as her fellow-creatures. Before long she came to imagine that a new mystery of simplicities had come to rejuvenate the world, and that she herself was an ordinary part of that mystery. Furthermore, because her presence had helped to create the mystery, it seemed to the self-conscious Dryad that she herself was to some extent the owner of it. Was she going insane? No! She was learning to recognize the very essences of earth, and wind, and water. Night was increasing her power.

Suddenly a bird squawked in a tree, and Stephanie formed the mental picture of a marauding snake.

On the margin of the lake, bulrushes began to rustle, for a new wind had arisen. *I am the breath of a bridge that links spring with summer*, it said. The tall girl listened intently. Did this new wind carry hints of a distant music?

She could feel an alteration in the structure of her mystery. The bones of her head seemed to be adjusting themselves to a new atmosphere. Was it possible, she asked herself, that some unseen hand was making a different arrangement of the particulars of her world? Was some hidden painter bringing about a significant change in the details of his picture? And if so, would the altered artwork be less hospitable to her than what had preceded it?

Go into the forest, said the wind. *Don't be content to stroll around the border of a true reality. You will learn more if you go further.*

Stephanie ardently embraced her tree, and went into the forest.

The path ended after about two hundred paces, but she walked on steadily, welcoming the insidious brambles that caught at her ankles, laughing when nettles brushed the sides of her calves, promiscuously hugging the trunks of stranger-trees, and luxuriating in the all-pervasive wind.

Above her head she could hear the murine squeaks of pipistrelles.

By some sonic alchemy, the hunting-song of the bats gave birth in Stephanie's mind to a thrilling piece of knowledge. She was not very far from a clearing.

I've never been happier, or more intensely alive, she thought. I want to be here more than anywhere. I need *to be touched by briars and nettles. I* need *to wrap my arms and legs round trees. I* need *the wind. I'm not cold. I've been far colder in a drenched hockey-kit. Wind, dear! Blow as hard as you like.* Stephanie was amazed when her almost frivolous prayer was answered at once. The wind increased noticeably in strength. *I want you,* it said. *So do the trees, and so do the plants that grow along the ground. We all want you.*

She kissed a young elm, and then walked towards the north. In this part of the wood the briars were thick and strong. Every few steps she lost her footing, and fell. At one point she noticed that her left knee was bleeding.

After seven minutes of very slow progress, Stephanie reached the foreknown clearing, and realized that the wind had died. An utterly barbaric thought entered her mind. *If I had brought a sharp knife with me, we could have sacrificed Victoria, and then the wind would have come back to life.*

What was that? Could it be – ? Yes! Again the boxwood saxophone was sounding in her mind. It was playing a melody which she found enchantingly primitive. She was afraid that the melody would last for only a short time.

Oooohhhh! Now she almost wished that she had never heard it in the first place. The raucous saxophone had awakened a furious yearning at the untilled centre of her being. In comparison with its music, nothing seemed worth while. The only thing that she wanted was to keep on hearing the savage music for ever and ever.

There it was again! Stephanie stood taut, alert, and entranced. She tried to breathe silently, but after a minute the music went on its way, so that she strained to hear it. Oh, the beguiling swagger of it! The proud, ebullient bellow!

The insistent, demanding, probing call of the saxophone! Stephanie had never heard such a tune in her dreams. The call of the melody was far more powerful than the timbre of its notes. With a delicious shiver of fear the Dryad realized that both the melody and the call were addressed to herself. It was likely, she thought, that the other girls could hear only a wind singing in the bulrushes on the margin of the lake. Captivated, transfixed, and palpitating, she herself was overpowered by the unknown saxophonist who had taken possession of her yielding soul. She fed on his distant melody like a trustful child who accepts the gift of a sweet from a friendly stranger.

Moonlight filtered through the trees on to the earth, and shone back at Stephanie from two pairs of eyes. Two little badgers were regarding her with cautious interest. Beside them, at the foot of an ancient hawthorn, stood a mushroom Stephanie was able to discern the precise nature of that mushroom more clearly than any well-behaved good girl who went to bed at ten thirty. *I have done well to stay awake for a third night*, she thought.

As if in disapproval, a bird whose voice she had already heard spoke for a second time. 'Mush-room, mush-room, snaaaaaaaaake!' it squawked urgently. 'Snaaaaaaaaake!'

At once the melody returned. Stephanie smiled, and walked on. Against the music of her wise saxophonist, the poor gibbering bird sounded like a punctured side-drum in the hands of a village idiot. Oooohhhh! She could never have imagined the melody whose phrases were crashing like breakers on the shore of her mind. The glorious tune was so real, so full of gravity, that it swallowed up the squawking bird, and turned its warning into a joke.

Was some rich green rite in progress? Stephanie had become a willing neophyte, and she was proceeding along a venerable path! Her ankles were courted now not by prehensile briars, but by the benign stems of purple loosestrife that bordered the timeless path on either side. The soles of her feet received a frank welcome from the roots of trees which ran in diagonal lines across the ancient path. She herself was not following some new-found path. The eternal path was drawing her onward. So was the primeval melody of her saxophonist. In fact, the old swinger was imposing his will upon her.

On moonlit patches of earth she was able to discern different forms of life. (The folded-up shamrock-leaves of wood sorrel. A pert group of polypodies. The creamy-white flowers of meadowsweet. A carpet of willowherb.) Stephanie began to sense that she was moving towards the climax of her dark expedition. The sacred hour was about to come, the hour for which she had been chosen! And the beings who had selected her were much more potent than the bespectacled drama teachers who had called her to work with Roderigo Maschera. Without haste, without hesitation, she continued on her course, like a serene hierophant, in a mood of tingling piety. Her feet had for some time been enjoying a most amiable relationship with the moist and mossy earth. How would she ever be able to wear shoes again?

The sacred hour had come for Stephanie, and she herself had come to the sacred place. It was right that her feet were unshod, because the ground on which she stood was holy. Here was the ordained theatre where her saxophonist had chosen to perform on his boxwood instrument. Here, and nowhere else, she would discover him.

Suddenly she was overwhelmed by a feeling of dread. Her long athletic legs began to tremble. A colossal strength was compelling the ivy-clad Stephanie to stand still, to bow her head, and to close her eyes.

It was neither a decorous nor a wholesome strength.

It was a hideous strength, with no love or joy or kindness about it. It was the strength of a cruel and destructive being.

Stephanie wished fervently that the other girls would lead her away to safety.

She tried to call out, but the strength had set a fiendish lock upon her throat.

And the music had stopped dead. So had all the little sounds of night. Some insolent person was exulting in his notional rights of ownership.

He really believes that he owns me, the incredulous girl said to herself.

The thought that any created being might presume to *own* her made Stephanie very angry. It was pure honest fury that enabled the girl to straighten her neck, to open her eyes, and to scrutinize the person who sat on a fallen tree in front of her. She regarded that person with fear, but not with awe.

She looked into the very countenance of the Enemy and the Destroyer.

She observed the gold-painted horns of a ram which had been made into a crude diadem. Even a scarecrow might have refused to wear such a crown.

She perceived the scornfully flared nostrils, and wondered if they served as cooling vents for the person's restless, red-hot eyes.

She was surprised by the carefully manicured beard. (Here was a fastidious razor-artist like her English teacher, Mr Faughan. In other words, here was a self-important person who spent a lot of his day in front of a mirror.)

She saw the wasted muscles of an old man's arm.

(Did she hear, or did she imagine, the wheezing that came from the wreckage of two lungs? How had those lungs been able to fuel a musical instrument?)

She noticed that the hand which held the little saxophone was wizened, and studded with black wens.

The shaggy goat's limbs brought two words of Shakespeare into her mind – *shrunk shank* – and with those two words came the death of her fear.

'Am I afraid?' she asked herself. 'Afraid of *him*? No, never! Oh, I know he's far stronger than I am, and I know he's far more intelligent than I am, and I know he could kill me if he wanted to, but I'm not afraid!'

In truth Stephanie was not afraid. Her chief emotion was disgust.

What was the most disgusting thing about the creature who sat in front of her? The fact that he expected to be worshipped.

The whole business was ridiculous.

Was it even real?

Stephanie was a rational being. It was within the bounds of possibility that the centre of a forest might be the lodging-place of a tramp. But there, regarding the tall girl as if he had bought her in a shop, was a fool who had fallen far below the level of a louche and leering tramp.

By the standards of her generation, Stephanie had a rich vocabulary for a girl of eighteen. The most obscene thing about the person, she thought, was the proprietorial arrogance in his eyes. *Kneel*, he seemed to say. *Kneel*.

'No,' Stephanie replied. 'I reject you. And there's nothing that you can do.'

Once she had spoken, the girl discerned a fatal wound on the person's head.

She turned her perfect back of polished flint on the ugly person. He reminded her of a malignant wasp which had tried to sting her on the last Saturday of November, when she was painting the inside of the greenhouse. The old wasp had been very angry, because it realized that it had only a short time to live.

Beyond the sylvan darkness Stephanie could see a tiny patch of moonlit water. It was the lake! Slowly and deliberately, she made her way back towards it. She heard no sound of pursuit. Twice she thought of looking back. Something stopped her each time. *You've rejected him*, it said. *Keep going*.

When the wind arose once again, Stephanie heard it as itself, and not as the vehicle of a lunatic message. What had happened to her? Had she prepared herself to see the person by taking herself with gruesome seriousness? Or by working herself up into a state of frantic self-consciousness?

In reply to her questions there came a sentence from some author whose name she had forgotten. *When I became a man, I put away childish things, including the fear of childishness and the desire to be very grown up.* Well, that sounded sensible! Stephanie addressed the wind in robustly childish terms.

> Oh, Wind, you're very rough today,
> You blow the clouds along,
> You puff my chimney smoke away
> And sing a windy song.
> You shake the washing to and fro,

You make me dance and sing,
You take my little bell and blow
To make it jingle-jing!
Jingle-jingle-jingle-jing!
Oh, it is a happy thing
To have a little bell to ring!

Seven words which a green-blooded Dryad might have found enigmatic – *You shake the washing to and fro* – hit Stephanie's mind like the notes of a shell-trumpet. There was more to washing clothes than soaking them in soapy water, rinsing them, and letting them dry on a line. As well as being dried by the wind, the clothes were freshened and invigorated. Being shaken to and fro was part of the cleansing process.

Very good! But what Stephanie needed right now was water, not wind. Once she reached the lake, she realized how much she had suffered from rapacious briars. With a faint sense that healing was often a matter of cleansing, she walked into the water, and began to swim.

A weekend to which she had looked forward for months had ended in horror.

As the cool fluid encompassed her, Stephanie tried to account for what she had seen. She had neither wanted nor expected to see the person. Had his appearance been a hallucination? Had the whiskey disordered her reason? She couldn't answer either question. But she would never drink alcohol again.

And she would never find it possible to dress up as a Dryad again.

Or as anything else.

She would never act again.

Stephanie didn't want to end up as the property of other beings.

She didn't want to belong to an agent. Or to a producer. Or to an audience. Or even to a fan club.

She might as well belong to that person back in the wood.

No one in the future was ever going to regard her as that person had done.

No one was going to exercise seigneurial rights over her.

On Monday she would go to her careers mistress.

After swimming until she was painfully cold, Stephanie came out of the water. She ran thirty-seven miserable circuits of the lake. When she felt warm and dry, she lay down on the pine needles, and looked up sadly at the sky. The one thing that she had wanted to do for two years was no longer desirable.

I am ME, she thought. *If I set myself to gratify people who think they own me, I shall diminish myself.*

She had wrongly believed herself to be in charge of events. Although she had organized tonight's little adventure, and commanded the obedience of her new friends, the person had been in control all along. What a deceiver! He had pretended to address her in the name of innocent trees, and innocent wind.

Stephanie remembered a piece of etymology from her Thursday Latin class. 'Person' was a theatrical word. It came from the Latin *persona* – the one who 'personated' or 'sounded through' the mask. Long ago, the person had 'sounded through' a snake. Snaaaaaaaaake!

At five o'clock Stephanie went back into the lake. Standing in three feet of water, she turned six well-known lines of Poe into music.

> By a route obscure and lonely
> Haunted by ill angels only,
> Where an Eidolon, named NIGHT,
> On a black throne reigns upright,
> I have wandered home but newly
> From this ultimate dim Thule.

One by one, over the next twelve minutes, fifteen other girls came and joined Stephanie in the lake.

They moved round and round in joyless circles, like goldfish in a bowl.

As if trying to blot out the memory of a nightmare, they swam for most of the time with their faces held down in the water.

Each Dryad had seen something dreadful, but the horror was too recent for her to speak of it today. Over the next few weeks, the girls would share their experience in letters and phone calls.

One reasonable idea came to all sixteen of the Dryads, filtering its way through their sorrow and their exhaustion. Whether or not she ever encounters Pan-like beings, a full-time nymph must lead a horrendously boring life.

The girls swam steadily until they noticed a strange glow in the east. For a moment Stephanie was bemused. Did the glow betoken some kind of aurora borealis? Then the truth erupted in her mind, and she called out excitedly to the other girls. All sixteen of them watched the glow deepen till their eyes, so long accustomed to lunar light, baulked a little at the sight. Two minutes later a strip of the lake's surface flushed into blood-red. It seemed to the girls that the glow from the east was running across the earth to greet them. A blade of real daylight made a path in the forest. Two starlings felt its advent, and filled the air with a noisy hymn of thanks. The sun had come back to the world.

At once the authentic humanity of the girls began to assert itself. They were hungry! On Saturday morning they had eaten very little for breakfast, but today they were going to take everything that was going – orange juice, grapefruit, cereal with milk, porridge with golden syrup stirred into it, bacon, eggs, tomatoes, hot buttered toast with marmalade, and hot, hot, hot tea.

They began to swim on their backs, kicking up a spray of gemmeous droplets behind them. Soon they were frolicking about like infants in a paddle-pool.

At six o'clock the Archdryad led them out of the lake. 'I've *never* had a night like that,' she said. 'Let's run round the lake till we're dry.'

Ten minutes later, believing that all of her friends had gone back to the centre, Stephanie exhumed a little bottle. She walked for a hundred paces, rejoicing in the warm sunlight, and spoke to herself. 'If it's growing anywhere,' she said, 'it ought to be growing here.'

'Oooohhhh.' The girl from Glasgow opened her eyes, and sat up slowly. She stared at the Archdryad, who was standing on the near bank of the lake's inlet stream 'I beg your pardon, what did you say, dear?' asked Victoria.

'I was wondering,' said Stephanie thoughtfully, 'if there might be watermint growing here. It's exactly the right sort of place for watermint. And look, Victoria! There it is!' With a cry of delight she jumped over the stream, and pounced upon a patch of purple-stemmed mint-plants.

The Scottish girl closed her eyes again. Having wakened from a terrible dream, she was now barely able to recall it. When a querulous calf mooed in a distant field, she smiled like a child. The dark vestigial terrors that survived in her memory were being annihilated by some strong and healthy thing.

What exactly was the thing? What was going on? Victoria opened her eyes.

Stephanie was holding a crushed sprig of watermint under her friend's nostrils. 'Let's catch up with the others, dear,' she said. 'I want *clothes*.'

For more than an hour the sixteen girls used hot water with reckless extravagance. There was much washing and combing of hair.

So ended a truly dramatic weekend. The Dryads ate a hearty breakfast, exchanged addresses with each other, and departed with their teachers. Most of the girls slept like Princess Aurora until they found themselves on home ground once again. Stephanie was returned to her family at a little after six o'clock. With a hockey-player's relish she ate nearly half of a large beef cobbler. Then she went to sing in the church choir.

'Now let's perform the first scene,' her teacher was saying. (Hooohhh! It was Monday, and the former Archdryad, whose briar-torn legs felt as if they were on fire, was reading a rather lurid article about sleep deprivation.) 'Can I have volunteers for the three witches?'

Stephanie surprised Mr Faughan by raising her hand at once. *She must have been listening after all*, he thought.

Before long the break-bell sounded. Coffee-time!

For the first time in almost fourteen years, Miss Owen rejoiced in the security of a school uniform.

She amazed her classmates by eating a chocolate bar.

On Tuesday, she resolved, she would write a full account of her recent doings, and send it to her uncle in Belfast.